HAZY GROOMS AND HOMICIDES

A RAINA SUN MYSTERY

ANNE R. TAN

Author's Note: This is a work of fiction. Names, characters, places, and incidents are a product of the author's imagination. Locales and public names are sometimes used for atmospheric purposes. Any resemblance to actual people, living or dead, or to businesses, companies, events, institutions, or locales is completely coincidental.

To Carol,
Love you, baby sister.

TIGHTY WHITIES

"Are you sure there are no more tickets for the Rock and Jam Convention?" Raina Sun asked. "My grandma has been pacing the floor in the hotel room. She would love the chance to dress up as Elvis Presley and strut her stuff with you all." She held her hands together as if in prayer. "Please. Pretty please." She was more than willing to grovel for her grandma's sanity...and her own.

"We're completely booked. There's not even standing room in the main hall." The organizer wore an orange lanyard with a name badge that indicated her name was Claire Boucher. Her clear blue eyes were apologetic, but the set of her mouth said she wasn't bending the rules.

Claire tucked a strand of gray-streaked red hair behind her multi-pierced ear. Half-moon reading glasses hung off the collar of her blouse, but her face was unlined and only had a hint of crow's feet at the corners of her eyes. She moved her phone aside and riffled through the stacks of paper on the plastic table in front of her with the frantic and frazzled air of a dog rooting for a chicken bone in the trash.

With over eight hundred convention attendees in the hotel-casino along with the guests, everyone was more irritable at the longer lines at the restaurants and the increased wait time for services. And the people running the convention probably had to deal with all the complaints. No wonder Claire looked frazzled, but Raina wasn't doing much better either.

Raina had to sit tight with two senior citizens and a service dog. Matthew, her fiancé, had left with his Jeep to finish up his freelance security gig days ago. He had promised her a good time, and she came to Las Vegas secretly hoping they would elope at one of the wedding chapels.

Instead, he had come and gone at all hours of the day—and night. And she had been stuck entertaining two senior citizens and walking the service dog. Matthew's grandma was no problem, but Raina's grandma was in a whole other league. And this Rock and Jam Convention was Raina's last ditch effort to keep from killing her grandma.

Raina grabbed a brochure from the table and scribbled her name and cell phone number on it. "I'm in Room 218. If a spot opens, please contact me. We're here for a few more days, so my grandma can fill in at any time."

Claire glanced at the brochure and blinked. "Raina

Sun. What an unusual name." Her gaze focused on Raina for the first time. "And curly black hair on a Chinese woman. Is it natural?"

Raina blushed. She was used to outspoken little old Chinese ladies, but Claire wasn't old enough to be a senior citizen. Raina couldn't help it if she looked like a pencil with an Afro. Her hair's moisture balance was off from the desert heat outside and the indoor air conditioning.

"Yes, it's natural. Curly hair is a recessive gene, but it pops up in my family now and then," she said, hoping she didn't sound too testy.

Claire flicked a glance at Raina's hand. "As long as your fiancé is okay with it, what does it matter."

"Matthew loves my hair."

Claire nodded absentmindedly. "I need to check in the people behind you."

Raina wanted to grovel some more but backed away instead. She didn't want to ruin any chance she might have of snagging a ticket. "Thank you for your time." Before she could turn away, someone brushed against her arm and got in front of her.

"Hi, Claire. It's Gloria Tanaka…"

Raina sidestepped out of the way and glanced over. This Gloria person was dressed as Cher and clutched her name badge like it was the last fried won ton on the plate. Whatever happened to personal space?

Claire paled. "What are you doing here?"

"I love rock-and-roll. Now where is the data you stole from my computer?" Gloria said.

Raina lingered next to the sign-in table. Stolen information? Cool. This was much better than returning upstairs to hang out with the grandmas.

Gloria's mouth twisted into a snarl. "You saw me log in with my password. If you don't come clean, not only will I lose my job, I could lose my security clearance for compromising the mission. I will never work at NASA again."

"I'm on vacation right now, so I don't want to think about work," Claire said. Her tone was pleasant but not friendly. She handed Gloria a welcome packet. "I have to check the rest of the people in."

"You can't get rid of me this easily," Gloria said. "I'm going to the Inspector General's office—"

The commotion at the end of the line grew louder. Raina glanced at the crowd. A man approached the folding table, winged by several people. All of them were wearing name badges from the convention. If Raina didn't know any better, she would have thought they were a lynch mob.

When they got close enough for Raina to see their angry faces, she backed away from the folding table and flattened herself against the wall. She crabwalked along the wall and edged around the group.

The leader of the group flattened his hands on the folding table and thrust his face forward. He looked like he was in his mid-forties with dark sideburns that might be real, unlike the thick toupee that sat at a jaunty angle on his head. He was a slight man, probably five foot seven, though his blazing pale blue eyes made him seem formidable. "Claire, where is the breakfast spread for the Sunset Room?"

Claire stiffened. "Good morning, Brian. Have you tried talking to the hotel staff before coming here with your friends to accuse me of failing to do my job?"

People in their rock band outfits drifted over and divided themselves between Claire and Brian. It looked as if even a convention had its share of politics. Gloria Tanaka grabbed her welcome packet, spun on her heels, and stomped off. She probably knew this wasn't the time to continue their conversation.

Raina was disappointed. Stolen data from NASA sounded more exciting than a missing breakfast spread. She edged away from the confrontation. She didn't think the convention attendees would exchange blows, but she didn't want to be stuck in this hallway until the crowd dispersed. She breathed a sigh of relief when she reached the casino floor.

Maybe signing her grandma up for the convention was a bad idea. Her grandma had a way of fanning the flames. And after several days of being cooped up in a hotel room without her usual cronies from the senior center, her grandma was more than ready for a little heat.

RAINA'S EYES POPPED OPEN, but she didn't dare move a muscle. Her gaze shifted around the hotel suite, looking for the source of the noise that woke her in the pre-dawn light. When she went to bed a few hours ago, she had locked the door but didn't use the swing bar lock in case Matthew returned later. She took a deep breath but didn't smell the clean water and sage body wash favored by her fiancé. Instead, there was a hint of gardenia and lilac in the air. A woman's perfume. Was there a woman in the room?

A bead of sweat trickled down the side of Raina's forehead. Her tight muscles ached. Fight or flight? Warrior or possum? Who was this woman in her room? It was five in the morning. Much too early for housekeeping. And not late enough for burglary. This intruder must think the suite was empty, which meant this woman knew Matthew...or knew his whereabouts.

Raina flipped off the covers and tiptoed to the dresser. She grabbed the pepper spray from her purse and tiptoed to the bedroom doorway. Taking a deep breath, she ran headlong toward the woman with her shoulder down as if ready to tackle her to the ground, screaming like a banshee. She could apologize later if the intruder turned out to be a friend.

The intruder spun around and gasped, reaching for the doorknob.

Raina stopped short at the terrified expression on Claire Boucher's face. She stumbled on the carpet. What was the convention organizer doing in her room?

Claire flung open the door and shot out of the room.

Raina ran after her, pumping her arms and legs to keep up. Running on a treadmill in the hotel fitness room didn't give her the same thrill as running on solid ground. And a chase really got her heart pumping. "Hey, Claire! Stop."

A door clicked open in front of her. Po Po popped her head out of the doorway. "Rainy? What are you—"

Raina didn't wait for her grandma to finish the question.

The hallway was empty, so there was nothing to slow their race. Instead of heading for the elevators, Claire headed for the staircase. Raina hoped they were heading down rather than going up the staircase. Her lungs began to burn, and her legs ached. She ignored both sensations and clattered down the stairs after the woman.

"Stop! I won't hurt you," Raina wheezed. At the moment she didn't have the energy to swat a fly.

Claire ignored her and kept running. She hopped down the last two steps and opened the door to the casino floor. For a middle-aged woman, she was in good shape.

Raina's foot crunched on something, and she stumbled in her stride. She grabbed the rail in time to stop from pitching headfirst down the stairs. She glanced down. It was one of Claire's earrings.

Half a heartbeat later, she flung open the door to the casino and ran out. The slot machines clanged even at this early hour. The lights were too bright, and several people were still gambling away. Raina spun around in a circle but couldn't see the woman.

Her breath came out in audible puffs, and her eyes

scanned the open area in front of her. The early morning gamblers watched Raina from the corner of their eyes. One man openly leered at her. Jerk.

Po Po waved and trotted towards her. Her grandma's silvery hair with red streaks in it was smashed up on one side and curled like a duck's tail on the other. Her dark brown eyes sparkled with mirth even in this early hour. Looped over one arm was a white bathrobe.

Raina put her hands onto her hips, resting her hands on...her bare flesh. What the—

Heat rose to her face. This couldn't be happening. She blinked, but her bare feet didn't disappear. She had run after Claire in her sleeping attire—a tank top and her underwear.

Every camera on the casino floor was probably enjoying the show. If only the floor would open at this moment and swallow her. The more she thought about it, the more horrified she felt. What if the general manager found out? This would reflect so poorly on her fiancé, who was hired by the casino to look into their security system.

Someone cleared her throat.

Raina glanced up from her toes. Her grandma held out the white bathrobe, and Raina put it on. The two of them headed for the elevators.

"Head up high, Rainy. Move like a queen," Po Po said.

Raina kept her head down. Easy for Po Po to say. Her grandma had on a T-shirt and yoga pants.

When the doors slid closed, Po Po started chuckling. She covered her mouth with her hands. The chuckles turned into a full belly laugh.

Raina's face burned, but the corner of her lips twitched. No doubt about it—her life was a sitcom. At least there were no holes or stains in her underwear. She had to be thankful for the small stuff, right?

Po Po followed Raina back into the suite she shared with Matthew and flopped down on the sofa in the sitting room. "Okay, what was that about? Who's that woman?"

Raina studied the entertainment unit. She opened the cabinet door. "Claire Boucher. She's the organizer for the Rock and Jam Convention," she called out over her shoulder. "When I woke up, she was searching for something here."

Po Po's eyes glowed. "Were you able to get me a ticket? The convention is like the West Coast version of Nashville squeezed into a week. Amateur musicians, talent agents, and fans. Live music twenty-four seven in the various rooms." She sighed. "It's heaven."

Raina gave her grandma an apologetic smile. "Sorry. It was full."

Her grandma sighed again. "Oh, well. At least we got this little mystery to solve. It's not murder, but it's better than nothing. I wonder if she was drunk. Wouldn't it be smarter to wait until midday to break into a hotel room? And she should have put on a pair of pantyhose over her face."

"Do criminals still do that? Most women I know don't bother with pantyhose anymore. Maybe pantyhose is blasé for criminals too," Raina said. "Besides, if she had walked down the hall with a pair of pantyhose over her face, the hotel security would be all over it."

Raina didn't think for a moment this was a burglary. Claire had moved with practiced ease like she had formal training with espionage or was a career criminal.

Po Po frowned. "I wonder why she targeted your room. Seems rather random."

Raina gave her grandma a sideways glance. While the room was under Matthew's name, she had written down the room number for Claire. Did Claire recognize Raina's name? And what was she looking for in the room? The door lock wasn't jimmied, so she must have a key card.

"I don't think it was random," Raina said and explained her logic. "I wish Matthew had told me what he was doing for the casino. What if this has to do with his work?"

Po Po nodded. "Speaking of your fiancé, when was the last time you spoke to him?"

"Two days ago. I'd expected Matthew to work, but I didn't think he would disappear." Raina hoped she kept the worry from her voice.

Po Po glanced at the smartwatch on her wrist. "Let's rendezvous for an early breakfast in an hour. And once we've got Maggie settled for the morning, we should talk to the General Manager."

Raina hesitated. As much as she would like to talk to someone in the hotel-casino, she was afraid of barging in on Matthew's work. Her fiancé might have good reasons for his disappearance. "Let's go talk to Claire first. This would give Matthew some time to get in touch. But let's not say anything to Maggie. I don't want her to worry."

"Rainy, I hate to break it to you, but grandmas always worry about their grandchildren. Maggie is no exception."

Raina suppressed a sigh. Yeah, she figured as much. The last thing she needed was two grandmas breathing down her neck while she searched for her missing fiancé in Sin City.

2

———

THE SOUP THICKENS

After breakfast, Po Po took Maggie Louie back to the hotel suite they shared. Matthew's grandma was sight impaired and preferred to spend time in front of the TV—listening to the Chinese drama shows streamed through her tablet and knitting—than to wander around in unfamiliar places.

Raina took the service dog for several walks around the block and made sure he did his business. By the time they went upstairs, the dog was ready for his chew toys and TV. She set a bottle of water and several chewy granola bars on the side table next to her future grandma-in-law and kissed her cheek. She checked the food and water bowls in the mini kitchen area.

Po Po was beckoning at the open door of the hotel suite. "Come along, Rainy. Adventure waits for no one."

The two of them took the elevator down to the casino floor and made a left toward the convention area. Outside the main hall, several Elvis Presley impersonators were playing together to a small crowd of other rock star impersonators that Raina didn't recognize.

Po Po made a beeline for the crowd. "Come get me when you're done," she called out over her shoulder.

Raina rolled her eyes. So much for her wing woman.

As she approached the plastic table on the side, her gaze scanned the area, looking for Claire Boucher. There was no sign of the convention organizer, but the woman who bumped into her yesterday was handling the table. She was still dressed in the Cher costume. For a moment, Raina wondered if the convention attendees wore their costume the entire week. Yuck.

She smiled at the Cher impersonator. Now, what was her name? Anne? Gloria? Yes, that was it. "Hi, Gloria, I'm looking for Claire Boucher. Is she around?"

Gloria straightened the stack of brochures advertising rock-and-roll collectibles. She was in her mid-thirties, and her almond-shaped brown eyes were heavily shadowed with white glitter makeup. She towered over Raina in her platform boots.

When she spoke, she showed yellow-stained crooked teeth. "No one has seen Claire since dinner. I volunteered to fill in for a bit, but it's almost my turn on the stage. I'm a dancer."

Raina blinked. How much dancing could someone do in four-inch platform boots? "Claire left a message on my phone. Two spots opened up after everyone checked in yesterday. I paid for the tickets online as soon as I heard the message. I thought she would have my welcome packet here."

"Like I said, no one could find her this morning."

"Did someone check her room? What room is she in?"

Gloria shrugged. "No idea. I'm not part of the inner circle of the planning committee." She dug under the table and pulled out two blank name badges. She slid them across the table with a permanent marker. "I don't know where the welcome packets are, but at least you can get inside the convention rooms now."

Raina's grin widened. This was as easy as taking candy from a baby.

"Do you have the confirmation email?" Gloria asked.

Raina cringed inwardly. She pulled out her cell phone and scrolled through her email until she found a PayPal receipt for a pair of shoes she had bought online. She flashed the phone display. "Here's the PayPal receipt."

Gloria flicked a perfunctory glance at the screen and returned to straightening the table. "Don't forget Talent Night is Saturday. There is a thousand-dollar cash prize for the best impersonator show."

Raina thanked Gloria and turned to search for her grandma. This was amazing! Now both she and her grandma could wander through the convention to search for Claire. She was probably inside one of the conference rooms, hoping to avoid Raina. After all, she had to expect Raina would come looking for her.

As Raina and Po Po wandered the exhibit and various convention halls, they scanned the crowd, though it was hard to recognize anyone in the sea of sequins, wigs, and flashy guitars.

Po Po grabbed Raina's forearm. "Look!" She pointed at a dark-skinned man with a thin mustache.

Raina squinted. Must be pretty good makeup to turn a woman into a man. "Are you sure that's Claire?"

"No, that's Little Richard." Po Po's eye glowed. "I must get his autograph." She made a beeline for the impersonator.

Raina tugged at her grandma's hand. "Whoa! This isn't a sightseeing expedition. Besides, these are wannabes, not the real deal. We're here to look for Claire Boucher."

"I don't even know what the woman looks like. When she ran by, I only got a glimpse of her dry hair. She needs a deep conditioning."

Raina suppressed a sigh. Trust her grandma to notice the most irrelevant detail. "This is like looking for a bean in a rice bin. Let's find the general manager. Maybe we can sweet talk him into giving up Claire Boucher's room number."

"Or he could tell us where in the world Matthew is," Po Po said, giving Little Richard a longing glance. "And then we'll need disguises to blend in with this crowd."

RAINA HAD EXPECTED Willie Machado to be a big beefy guy, someone that could be the bouncer at a nightclub. Yes, she was stereotyping, but this was Las Vegas.

Instead, the general manager was a busty five-foot-six tawny blonde with eyes the color of brandy. She wore a tight black pants suit, the kind a model might wear at a photo shoot, and three-inch stiletto pumps. When she spoke, she had the gravelly voice of a senior citizen who had been chain-smoking her entire life even though she was not a day over forty.

"What did you say his name was again?" Willie asked, her hands folded in front of her on the desk. The talon-like nails looked like a formable weapon a la Wolverine. A walkie-talkie and a closed file folder were the only two items in front of her.

"Elliott Matthew Louie," Raina repeated for the third time. She suppressed the urge to sigh. She didn't believe Willie was being difficult on purpose, but the general manager might have some unacknowledged hearing loss.

Raina reached into her purse and pulled out one of Matthew's business cards and slid it across the desk. "He's a homicide detective for Gold Springs, California, but sometimes he freelances. Someone contacted him a few weeks ago to hire him to check the security system for this hotel-casino. We've been here for three days already."

Willie picked up the card and studied it, flipping it

over to look at the back. "Never heard of him. We don't hire people off the street to work on our security system." She slid the card back across the desk.

"Matthew isn't someone just off the street," Po Po said. There was a hint of defensiveness in her voice. "He is an ex-Marine, worked for the FBI, and this security job came from a friend."

Raina patted Po Po's knee. When did Matthew work for the FBI? She dismissed the thought for another time. There was still so much she didn't know about her fiancé.

As much as she loved the defensiveness in her grandma's voice, she didn't want to irritate Willie. The general manager didn't believe the hotel-casino hired a consultant to check on their security system, and short of whipping out a signed contract, Raina didn't see how she could convince Willie otherwise. Time to explore a different path.

"One of the perks for the security job was the two suites. If the hotel-casino didn't hire Matthew, who paid for the rooms?" Raina asked.

Matthew had checked them in and handed Raina and the grandmas their key card, so she had no idea who booked the suites.

Po Po gave Raina a nod of approval.

Willie glanced at the smartwatch on her wrist. "Ladies, I have twenty pounds of fish sitting in ice chests outside the kitchen, a broken water main, and I have over eight hundred Elvis Presley impersonators walking around the hotel. I have to go." She stood and gestured at the door.

"Someone came into my room at five in the morning using a key card," Raina said, staying put on the chair. She wasn't leaving without some answers. "Does your front desk give out keys without checking identification?"

Willie's eyes narrowed. "Miss Sun, we always verify the identity before issuing key cards. You said five AM?" At Raina's nod, Willie's frown deepened. She picked up the walkie-talkie and spoke into it. When she finished her conversation, she addressed Raina. "My head of security will meet you outside my office. He can go through the video feed of the corridor outside your room."

Raina stood. Well, at least this was something. "Would the front desk be able to help me figure who booked our suites?"

Willie walked around her desk and stood next to the doorway of her office. "Their computers would have the information. And once they verify your identity, they should be able to help you."

As Raina and her grandma stepped out into the hallway, Willie's walkie-talkie crackled to life. Willie returned to her desk and turned up the volume knob. Raina and Po Po lingered at the doorway, waiting for security as instructed.

"...dead body...laundry room...call the police..."

Raina's pulse jumped at the message. A stranger in her room, and now a dead body in the service hall.

What were the odds? She hoped these events had nothing to do with Matthew, and until she had more information, it wouldn't hurt to keep her eyes and ears open.

Willie grabbed the walkie-talkie and pressed a button. "Willie here. Can you repeat what you said?" She glanced up to see both Raina and Po Po staring at her. As the message came through a second time, she closed the office door.

Po Po pressed her ear to the door. "I can't hear a thing." She scowled at the door. "Who do you think is dead? One of the employees? Or maybe the Mafia knocked off someone for the casino."

Her grandma's eyes glowed with excitement. Any minute now, her grandma would insist on checking out the laundry room. There were only so many hours a person could spend in front of the penny machine and the buffet line before the brain turned to mush.

Raina strolled toward the elevator. She was doing this for Matthew. After all, when he surfaced again, he might like to know what was happening in the hotel-casino.

Tell yourself what lies you need, girl, said a small voice inside her head.

Raina ignored the comment. She knew what she was doing. She didn't want to be the woman left behind waiting for her man. Any action was better than picking her belly button lint. And it wasn't like she was committing to investigate the death. She was just another lookie-loo. There were plenty of those at the scene of an accident.

"We should go check out the laundry room," Po Po said, trotting to keep up. "If Willie gets there before we do, she'll make us leave. We can always check in with security later. Claire Boucher isn't going anywhere with the convention in full swing."

"Why do you think we're power walking to the elevator?" Raina asked.

Po Po gave Raina a wide beaming smile. "That's my girl."

3

DIRTY LAUNDRY

It took Raina and her grandma fifteen minutes to find the service hall. They had to pretend to be new employees looking for the general manager. The first uniformed employee they asked gave them a suspicious look and directed them to one of the casino floor supervisors. The second employee was more trusting and gestured at the rear wall next to the buffet.

Raina and Po Po strolled through a set of unattractive double swinging doors and into the service hall with its own freight elevator. The carpeted floor became a beige tile. The wood wainscoting disappeared, and the walls were a drab off white. Even the lighting appeared dimmer as if someone in management was trying to save costs by cutting corners.

As Raina and Po Po approached the laundry room, there wasn't anyone in the hallway to keep out busybodies. From the doorway, Raina saw two industrial size washer and dryer sets and white laundry bags stacked in front of them. One bag was partially opened, revealing the victim's face.

Raina gasped. She staggered forward, grabbing onto the door frame for support. The victim was Claire Boucher. Raina's gaze shifted down from the face to the neck. Deep bruise marks circled her neck. Someone had strangled the poor woman.

She blinked several times, but the scene in front of her didn't disappear. The harsh fluorescent light of the laundry room washed out all the colors in the world, except for the victim's red hair. Stainless steel, white floors, white light, and red hair. Bile rose in her throat, and she swallowed several times but couldn't get rid of the taste in her mouth.

Po Po patted Raina's back. "Maybe we should get out of here." Her grandma's voice was unsteady. The hand on Raina's back shook.

Raina dragged her gaze away from the victim to glance at Po Po. Her grandma's ashen face snapped Raina out of her frozen position. They had to get out of here before her grandma passed out from the shock. She held onto her grandma's arm, and they turned away from the doorway of the laundry room.

"What are you two doing here?" someone snapped from behind them.

Raina's head jerked up.

Willie scowled at them. Next to her was a man in a crisp white shirt, black tie, and black suit. Everything about the man was square—square nose, square jaw, and a square tank of a body. He towered over the tawny blonde in her three-inch heels. His hooded dark brown eyes hid his emotion and thoughts. He would have made a good bouncer.

"We were heading out to my car." Raina pointed a shaky finger at the side entrance of the hotel-casino.

"Why...why is that woman in a laundry bag? Who...who was she?" Po Po asked. There was a tinge of hysteria in her grandma's voice.

Raina blinked at a sudden thought. Her grandma didn't recognize Claire Boucher, but the security team would have seen Raina chasing Claire on the video surveillance before the discovery of her body. The whole thing would make Raina a suspect. In the eyes of the security team, it would look like she had returned to the scene of the crime. Yikes! Coming down here was a serious mistake.

Willie eyed them and spoke over her shoulder. "Hendricks, I thought you posted a guard."

Hendricks pulled out his cell phone and tapped on it. "Let me find out." His phone chirped, and he glanced at the message. "She had to go to the ladies room."

"The pregnant one?"

"Yes."

Willie pressed her lips into a thin line.

Hendricks gave an apologetic shrug. "She's the only one available."

Willie rubbed the temple of her head. "Put Miss Sun and her grandma in the room with the maids.

They can't leave the crime scene until after the police speak with them."

Hendricks gestured for Raina and Po Po to follow him. His dark hooded eyes regarded them without any emotion. This was just business for the man. For a moment Raina wondered what other messes he might have cleaned up for the hotel-casino.

Raina straightened and stood her ground. She didn't want to be held in a cell like a criminal. After all, this was Las Vegas. How did she know this casino wasn't run by the mob? They got rid of problems by burying them in the desert sand. No siree. She was staying out here where someone could hear her scream.

"You have no authority to detain us," Raina said. She didn't want to sound confrontational, but she wasn't willing to be a chump either. "We're more than happy to cooperate with the police, but we'll stay right here."

"How do we know you're not connected to the mob?" Po Po asked.

Though Raina still didn't like her grandma's pale coloring, at least her voice sounded more like her normal self.

"We don't want to disappear." Po Po made air quotes around the last word. "I've seen the movie *Casino*."

Raina suppressed a smile. It looked like her feisty grandma was back, and on the same wavelength with Raina.

Willie rolled her brandy-colored eyes. "I don't have time for this nonsense. Just stay here and don't disturb anything."

Willie and Hendricks turned and went into the laundry room. They came outside almost immediately. Willie closed the laundry room door with a napkin from her pocket. Both of them were frowning with that determined look of professionals taking care of dirty business.

"Get someone to stand guard and wait for the police, Hendricks," Willie said. "And have someone posted outside the entrance to guide the police back here without going through the casino floors. I don't want to alarm any of our guests. Text me when the police get here. I need to call corporate."

Raina never gave much thought to the business side of the hotel-casino. Was corporate a code word for the mob or did Willie mean a head office somewhere like your average Fortune 500 company? This thought made Raina feel better. A corporation surely didn't bury bodies in the desert? So they were probably safe enough from the mob. And who put the idea of the mob in her head in the first place?

Willie strolled away, her heels clicking on the tile floor. Hendricks stood in front of the laundry door, feet spread, hands tapping on his cell phone. Probably to carry out the instructions issued by his boss.

Raina glanced around at the ceiling and noticed two security cameras in the middle of the service corridor, one pointing back to the main area and one pointing toward the laundry room and side entrance. Hopefully, the cameras recorded who was in the service hall with Claire at the time of her death.

But if the killer approached this corridor with his or her head ducked down, the second camera would only capture the person's back. If the person wore baggy clothes, security might not even be able to tell if the killer was male or female. Not much use in a murder investigation.

Raina shivered at the thought. There was no doubt someone had strangled Claire Boucher and stuffed her in a laundry bag between 5 AM when she was last seen running out of Raina's room and a few minutes ago. Would she have died if Raina didn't chase her out into the open? There was no way to tell, but Raina could not help but feel guilty for her contribution to Claire's demise.

At this point, the only thing she could do for the poor woman was to help track down the killer. She gave Hendricks a sideways glance. She whispered to her grandma in Chinese, "Distract him for me. I want to look around outside."

"I'm on it, Sherlock," her grandma mouthed.

Po Po staggered toward Hendricks, flapping a hand on her face. "Young man," she called out in a reedy voice.

Hendricks glanced up from his smartphone.

Po Po took two more steps and rolled her eyes upward. "I feel faint..."

Hendricks reached out automatically and caught

Po Po before she could collapse on the floor. Her grandma must have started acting lessons. As he turned to settle Po Po onto the ground, Raina slipped out the side entrance.

Once outside, she sidestepped to get away from the glass cut-out on the door in case Hendricks looked around for her. To her right was the loading dock where deliveries must come in daily to keep the restaurants and shops stocked. On the left was the concrete enclosure hiding the commercial trash bins. Next to it, a small concrete footpath led around the building. To escape, the killer wouldn't have gone toward the loading dock or the trash bins.

Raina followed the footpath, scanning the ground. Around the corner of the building, she found a white card poking up from the hedges next to a patch of towering holly oak trees. She got down on her hands and knees to peer underneath the bushes, reaching into her purse for a tissue. She pulled out the white plastic card. It was still attached to an orange lanyard. Did someone from the convention pass through here?

She flipped the card around. Brian Anderson. The man who confronted Claire about the missing breakfast spread. While this seemed like a weak motive for killing someone, if this animosity had gone on long enough, he could have snapped.

Raina returned the name badge to its original location underneath the hedge. She glanced around but didn't see any security cameras. What were the odds of Brian losing his name badge in this remote part of the hotel-casino on the same day Claire's body was discovered?

RAINA FOLLOWED the footpath until she found another entrance and slipped inside. The cool blast of the air conditioning greeted Raina, and her curly black hair fanned out behind her like she was on a photo shoot. She glanced up at the ceiling to find several security cameras. There probably weren't enough human resources to monitor every screen, but she assumed the security team was following her every move.

She headed to the nearest restroom and did her business. If Hendricks asked, she could truthfully say she was in the ladies' room. As she made her way across the casino floor and back to the service hall, she passed several women in tight white tops and short black skirts, holding out trays of drinks. These servers ignored Raina even though she could have used a cold drink.

Raina licked her parched lips. What she wouldn't give for a nice cold drink and maybe a nap back in her room. And as quickly as the thought flashed across her mind, a stab of guilt twisted her stomach.

Claire Boucher would never feel the summer heat on her skin again or taste a refreshing drink. Whatever she did to cause the killer to snap, Claire surely didn't deserve to die, not when hardened criminals walked among innocent people.

As Raina stepped through the double doors and approached the laundry room, Hendricks glanced up from his cell phone. From the set of his mouth, Raina knew he was annoyed with her. "Where have you been?"

"I had to go to the ladies room," Raina said, which was technically true. "Hendricks, my fiancé told me your security team hired him to help with your computer system. Is he watching us now?" She waved at the cameras on the ceiling, pretending like she was a bimbolina wanting to catch her man's attention.

"We don't hire contractors," Hendricks said.

"I thought a contractor for upgrades is cheaper than a full-time computer guy," Raina said. She cringed inwardly. Now she was really fishing. Someone had to know about Matthew in this place. Her fiancé wouldn't have lied to her. She just hoped he wasn't in a hole out in the desert.

Hendricks grunted and returned to tapping on his phone.

Raina didn't think he was on Facebook chatting with his friends. He was probably directing his staff to do something and used the text app for privacy.

Po Po was perched right next to his side. She squinted at his screen, but Raina couldn't tell if her grandma could actually read the tiny display. Since her cataract surgery a few years ago, she had better vision than Raina.

Every once in a while, Hendricks scowled in her grandma's direction and took a step sideways as if to put some distance between the two of them. Po Po pretended to blink at the ceiling and ignored his look. The senile old lady act again. And when he wasn't looking, she would inch closer to reduce the gap between them.

Wait a minute, Raina thought.

Her grandma thrust her chest at Hendricks's phone screen. Was the locket on Po Po's neck a tiny camera? Or maybe the sunflower pin on her designer T-shirt was the camera? Was her grandma taking pictures of Hendricks's screen to capture the conversation? One of Po Po's hands was tucked inside her pants pocket. She might be activating the camera's shutter with a remote.

There was a commotion behind Raina, and she spun around to see the police approaching—four uniformed officers and a detective in plain clothes. Raina thought they got here much too quick. Maybe the hotel-casino had some influence with the police department. After all, the city did have a history of misconduct in the police force.

Would they cover up this murder? No, it would be hard to cover something like this. Claire Boucher had probably been organizing the Rock and Jam Convention for years, so the attendees would notice and demand answers at her sudden death.

Or would the police do a slapdash investigation so the hotel-casino wouldn't get any bad publicity? This seemed the more likely route. Mishandling or contaminating the evidence could shelve the investigation pretty quickly. It seemed strange the forensic team wasn't dispatched with these officers. After all, didn't the security team from the hotel-casino tell the dispatcher that Claire Boucher was dead?

Hendricks glanced up from his phone and slipped it in his pocket. "Officers, I'm so glad you're here. When the general manager and I came downstairs, we found these two"—he jerked a thumb at Raina and her grandma—"in the laundry room with the victim. I don't know if they are witnesses or suspects."

Po Po glared at the security guard. "Witnesses, you big ape."

Hendricks ignored the comment and gestured at the laundry room. "The body's in there."

"We were supposed to meet with security about a separate issue," Raina said. "We heard he was down here, so we came down hoping to catch him. It sounds like we're not the first one to arrive on the scene. The maids found the body first."

Hendricks pulled out his walkie-talkie. "Let me know when you're ready to interview me." He stepped aside, probably to inform his boss the police had arrived.

An officer approached Raina and Po Po, and the rest filed into the laundry room. Raina wanted to groan out loud. Why would all four police officers need to go inside? It wasn't like the killer was still hiding inside when there was an exit a few feet away. All their shoes tracked in who knew what, and the extra skin cells would contaminate the entire crime scene.

The officer questioned Raina first, asking her to

step toward the exit so her grandma couldn't hear Raina's answers.

"Tell me what happened," the officer said.

Raina started with the walkie talkie in Willie's office and their discovery. She mentioned going around the building.

"Why did you go outside?"

"I was so cold after discovering the body." Raina shivered at the memory. "I needed to feel the warmth of the sun." The words rang true. She hadn't realized she had unconsciously sought out the heat. "Then I went to the ladies room."

"Have you seen the victim before?" the officer asked.

"Yes," Raina said reluctantly. "Her name is Claire Boucher, the organizer for the Rock and Jam Convention. I spoke with her yesterday about getting my grandma a ticket." Should she say something about chasing Claire down to the casino floor? It sounded so incriminating, though Raina had done nothing wrong.

Sometimes Raina wondered if her ancestors had a wicked sense of humor. They were supposed to look out for her, but she seemed to always end up in situations where dead bodies turned up.

She gave her grandma a sideways glance. Maybe Po Po had been praying for a distraction like this to get her through the week. Raina groaned at the thought. She needed to stop this circular logic. It was getting her nowhere.

The officer moved on to another question, and the

moment passed for Raina to say something about chasing Claire. She wasn't withholding information, just organizing it in her head until she had her facts straight. Besides, the detective in charge would probably want to speak to Raina again once the investigation was in full swing.

4

—————

BONUS FOR A CAPE

After Po Po's interview, the police let them go. They weren't told to stay in town, but Raina had a feeling they wouldn't like it if she left the city with the grandmas. She wanted to linger, but the combined glares of Hendricks and the police officer changed her mind. Po Po went to check on Maggie, probably to regale her best friend with news of the body discovery.

Raina returned to her suite, kicked off her shoes, and collapsed onto the bed. She lay there for several long moments, soaking in the silence. Even though the room was non-smoking, the air quality was only a tad better than the casino floor. After all, it wasn't like they had separate ductwork for the non-smoking rooms. She took several deep breaths anyway.

The Western theme hotel-casino was once considered top-of-the-line in its heyday thirty years ago. The cowboy theme continued into the rooms with colors of the desert—mute tans, beige, and accented with iron horseshoes. Now it was struggling to attract tourists against the more modern and expensive hotels on the Strip.

Given the age of the place, she had assumed Matthew was hired to modernize their security system, but she made the wrong assumption. Her fiancé was working on something else entirely. It was annoying that he didn't tell her about it, but maybe he didn't think it was worth going into the details. She reached in her purse for her cell phone and called Matthew. Just like last night, the call went straight to voice mail.

"Hi, love. I haven't heard from you in a few days, and I'm starting to get worried. Things have gotten strange here." Raina told him everything. "Like I said, strange happenings, and it makes me worry about you. Are you in trouble or something? Please call me back. I love you."

Raina hung up, feeling unsatisfied with the message, but she didn't know what else to do about it. Normally they had a habit of speaking every night and usually got in touch a few times a day, depending on the case he was working. Matthew must have believed this gig was a cakewalk to suggest Raina and the grandmas join him in Las Vegas. His absence and silence meant something went horribly wrong.

And to top it off, she secretly worried that Claire Boucher's murder might have something to do with his freelance gig. She had no reason to investigate the murder...except how could she explain to the police about chasing Claire down the staircase and onto the casino floor? Even now, Raina had no idea why the convention organizer was in her room in the first place. And if there was a possible link to Matthew...

Raina sat up on the bed. She should call the front desk and find out who was paying for their suite. She grabbed the landline on the side table and dialed zero. The phone rang twice, and someone picked up.

After the usual greetings, Raina asked, "What name is on the reservation for my suite? My fiancé handed me a key card when we checked in, but he didn't say if his employer paid for the room or if we're expected to pay when we check out."

She must have sounded plausible because she could hear the front desk clerk tapping on his keyboard. "The name on the reservation is Matthew Louie. He put down his Visa, but I can't tell if it's a business card or his personal card. Is there anything else I can help you with?"

Raina thanked the man and hung up. Her heart sank. Yep, the security upgrade was a cover story. Probably told only for Raina's and the grandmas' benefit. In other words, he didn't expect her to check up on the story...or his absence.

She curled up into a fetal position on the bed and silently shook. She had about an hour to get her act together before meeting the grandmas for dinner. On the surface, she had to appear like nothing was wrong when everything might be falling apart.

Despite what Po Po said, the two grandmas looked

to her to gauge whether or not to go into full-blown panic mode over Matthew's absence. He wouldn't appreciate her contacting the authorities if he were working undercover or hiding from the bad guys. And right now, she didn't have enough information to act. But luckily, asking nosy questions was her specialty.

RAINA WALKED Poe around the block and waited while he did his business. After checking to make sure the service dog had food and water, she scheduled a pick up with a rideshare app on her phone to a nearby Thai restaurant for dinner. The grandmas loved the idea of an outing since they were just as sick of the restaurant selection at the hotel-casino.

A few minutes later, they placed their orders with the server. A middle-aged man came by to inquire about the empty chair at their table.

"Sure, you can take it, but what do we get in exchange for it?" Po Po asked, her eyes twinkling with amusement. "Do we get a song and a dance?"

The man started gyrating his hips and pumping his arms to some invisible beat. "This good enough?"

"How about a little more booty?" Po Po said, clapping her hands.

The man promptly turned around and wiggled his flat butt. Half his crack was showing on top of his belt.

Raina groaned and slid further down in her seat. There wasn't enough bleach in this world to clean her eyes. A glance around the restaurant showed several people looking at them with open laughter.

Maggie Louie didn't say anything, but her open smile was enough to show her enjoyment of the scene. While Po Po was thin and hip, her best friend was well padded and looked like the proverbial granny who liked to bake and knit. Her long silver hair was pulled back into a bun and held in place with chopsticks. She opened her purse and handed Po Po several dollar bills. Raina could see why the two ladies had been friends for over fifty years. Maggie lived vicariously through Po Po.

"Just take the chair and go," Raina said, her face flaming. This was so embarrassing. Could they get arrested for stuffing money down his pants? Disturbance of the peace?

The man gave them a flourishing bow that could have made a court jester proud. He grabbed the chair and went to join his friends at a nearby table. His friends clapped and whooped when he returned with his prize.

After the server dropped off their meal, they went through the details of Claire Boucher's murder.

"So Brian Anderson is on the top of the suspect list, huh?" Maggie asked.

"His motive is a stretch for me. Would you kill someone over a missing breakfast spread?" Po Po asked.

"Yeah. I would kill someone if there's no coffee in the morning," Maggie said.

Raina's eyes widened. It had been years since she had spent as much time as she did with Maggie these last few days. She had always thought her second grandma was a sweet old lady.

At the look on Raina's face, Maggie laughed. "Just kidding. I might throw a fuss like a child, but I would only stab someone's hand with a fork." She exchanged a look with Po Po and the two ladies burst into laughter.

The ladies tried to explain the story. Something about a bacon shortage on a road trip decades ago, but Raina didn't get it. But what she got was a longing for a best friend to share a history. And she hoped Matthew could fill this role in their future.

"What about the NASA girl? What's her name?" Po Po asked. "I wonder if she's a rocket scientist."

Raina refocused on the discussion at hand. She pulled out a notebook and made some bullet points. She might as well get her thoughts organized. "Gloria Tanaka. She's upset because Claire stole information from her workstation. She could lose her job and reputation."

Po Po nodded. "That's our killer. Now we just need her to confess."

"I'm sure you can beat it out of her," Maggie said.

Raina shook her head. "No beatings. We'll ask her some questions like a civilized person."

The grandmas gave Raina a doubtful look.

After dinner, they got a ride back to the hotel-casino. Raina walked the grandmas back to their suite and bid them good night, but she was too jazzed up with nervous energy to go back to her room. She grabbed her name badge for the convention and headed downstairs. From the program, she knew the exhibit hall was open for another half an hour. Maybe someone down there would be willing to talk to her about Claire Boucher.

THE EXHIBIT HALL was one open space with pop-up booths in several rows. In the front of the hall was a raised stage with a rock band playing an '80s song that Raina didn't recognize. Her grandma probably could have named the band by the outfits they were wearing. To her right was a snack bar counter displaying pastries behind a glass case. For a moment, Raina wondered if leftover pastries would be served first in the morning. Groups in twos and threes still wandered among the booths—most of them in costume.

Raina had a hard time identifying any of them. She glanced down at her outfit. Her dragonfly print T-shirt and shorts stood out in this crowd and not in a good way. Even the attendants in the booths wore a costume or a T-shirt advertising their favorite band. Her grandma was right. They would need outfits.

She stopped at the nearest costume booth and searched the rack. Her criteria was simple—something that fit both her body and her wallet.

The saleswoman came over. She was about five

foot seven with emerald green eyes. Her white hair was braided and wrapped around the crown of her head. She had a pleasant, smiling face. "Are you looking for anything in particular?"

Before Raina could reply, a familiar voice cut in from behind her. "How about some sequined jumpsuits? Bonus points if there's a cape."

Raina spun around. "What are you doing here?"

Po Po wiggled her eyebrows. "I can't let you have all the fun. I followed you down here. We could have matching outfits and carry guitars."

The saleswoman nodded. "What size are you looking for?"

Po Po rattled off their sizes, and the saleswoman looked through another rack.

"Guitars? Aren't they big and bulky?" Raina whispered to her grandma.

Po Po shrugged. "Yeah, but they look cool. Besides, if we need to, we can hide a machine gun in the case."

Raina squeezed her eyes shut and rubbed the bridge of her nose. Now she remembered where she got the idea about the mob burying people out in the desert—her grandma's wild imagination at work.

The saleswoman reappeared and held up two costumes. One was a white polyester jumpsuit with gold trim and a gazillion crystals sown on the jacket. The other one was a red jumpsuit with golden sequins in the shape of pinwheels. "If you get both of them, I'll throw in the wigs for free."

Po Po's eyes glittered with excitement, and she

reached for the red jumpsuit. "Oh, yeah. My day just keeps getting better."

As if sensing an imminent sale, the saleswoman said, "Why don't you try it on? I have a dressing room in the corner." She pulled back the curtain to a dressing booth with a full-length mirror. Her grandma disappeared behind the curtain without further urging.

While her grandma dressed, Raina asked the saleswoman, "Do you know Claire Boucher? I've been looking for her all day. I'm having issues with my pass for the convention."

The saleswoman shook her head. "No, this is her first year putting together the show. Brian Anderson has been organizing the convention for over a decade, but he got pneumonia a few months ago. Claire was filling in for him. So I'm not surprised if there are issues. It seems like everyone is complaining about something this year."

Raina's ears perked up. "I know there was something wrong with the breakfast in one of the convention rooms yesterday. What other issues are there?"

"Some money from the ticket sales disappeared. No one knows what happened to it. That's why there's so much tension about the shortage of food and booze. As you know, the tickets for this event are not cheap."

"Did somebody embezzle funds?"

The saleswoman shrugged. "Who knows? Ten thousand dollars is a lot of money. They had to raise the booth prices in the exhibit hall to make up for it. I paid an extra two hundred dollars this year. It soured the weeklong festivities for us old-timers. I've been coming to this convention with my husband for over ten years."

"Are people blaming Claire?"

"I don't know. No one has seen her since last night. We tried calling her, but it went straight to voicemail. And someone said she lost her phone yesterday." The saleswoman shrugged. "Who knows what's going on? She could be on her way to Mexico with the money."

Raina's eyes widened. Was Claire killed because she stole the money? "What about Brian Anderson? Is he at the convention? What does he say about all this?"

"He's around here somewhere," the saleswoman said. "And of course he's not happy with what's happening. But there's nothing he can do about it. Claire had access to all the accounts while he was in the hospital."

Po Po came out and whirled in front of them. "What do you think?"

Raina wanted to push her grandma back into the dressing booth so she could continue her conversation.

The saleswoman gave her grandma two thumbs-up. "It looks great on you. I even have a red cape to go with it." She dug in a cardboard box underneath the display table and pulled out a mini cape. She draped it over Po Po's shoulders. The bottom rested at her grandma's waist.

Po Po stroked the fabric of the cape. "Ohhh! It's velvet. I like it."

"I don't know. Maybe you should try the white jumpsuit," Raina said, hoping her grandma would take the hint to go back into the dressing booth.

The saleswoman shook her head. "The red looks good on your granny. You should try out the white jumpsuit. It'll look smashing with your black hair."

Raina sighed. It looked like her info gathering session was over. She tried on the jumpsuit. When she turned her head, she had to do it slowly, or the big stiff collar might poke her eyes.

When Raina came out of the dressing booth, Po Po clapped. "We'll take them."

As Po Po paid for the outfits, Raina studied the program. Tomorrow morning, Brian Anderson would be hosting guitar troubleshooting lessons in the Sunset Room. It looked like her grandma might have her wish after all.

"Where can we rent guitars around here?" Raina asked, glancing up from the program.

Po Po did a fist pump. "Oh, yeah."

The saleswoman handed back Po Po's credit card. "Go straight to the front, the third booth on your left has instrument rentals. We get a lot of new guitar players in these events. The minimum rental period is three days."

They thanked the woman and made their way to the instrument booth. Raina told Po Po a summary of her conversation with the saleswoman and her plan to look for Brian in the morning.

"Yikes, it sounds like there is more afoot than just

the missing money," Po Po said. "I wonder if she hid the money in your room."

Raina considered the idea and dismissed it. "I would have noticed a wad of cash around the entertainment unit. Tomorrow will be interesting. The police might start questioning the convention attendees. Claire Boucher's death will be public knowledge by then. I wonder how Brian will react to the news."

"Then we better get to the seminar bright and early with a bowl of popcorn to watch the show," Po Po said.

They passed several booths selling authentic rock-and-roll memorabilia. Po Po almost made a detour inside a booth, but Raina held onto her grandma's arm. "We're here to work, not load up our suitcases."

Po Po harrumphed. "I don't have time at my age to work anymore. Everything I do is for pleasure."

Raina rolled her eyes. "I thought you were sixty this week. You still have plenty of time to become a hoarder. Come on."

At the instrument booth, her grandma put down a deposit and her credit card information. Luckily, Raina was able to convince her grandma to rent one guitar instead of two. As she lugged all the purchases to the elevator a few minutes later, she wondered if seeking out Brian Anderson in the morning was a good idea. After all, if the police showed up when Raina was at the seminar, the detective might want to question her too.

5

KISSING THE TOILET BRUSH

After a restless night, Raina took Poe out for a jog the next morning. The Strip was relatively safe enough, and a big black Labrador retriever running full tilt on a leash was a deterrent for most criminals. By the time she got back to the hotel-casino, the service dog was ready for his breakfast.

She returned to her suite for a shower and had scones and coffee with the grandmas at the café. They discussed their plans for the day, and once again, Maggie opted to stay in the suite to watch Chinese shows. Since her future grandma-in-law was listening to the shows rather than staring at the screen, Raina didn't object to the plan. It couldn't be any worse than listening to the radio all day. Maggie's hearing was sharper than ever, so no one could complain the retiree was ruining her ears.

An hour later, Raina was in the hallway outside

their room synchronizing her watch with Po Po so they could rendezvous in half an hour. She returned to her suite to change into her white jumpsuit costume. She was inside the bathroom stuffing her hair into the wig when someone knocked on the door.

"Housekeeping," came the muffled voice on the other side of the door.

Raina came out of the bathroom. The door opened a crack, and a stout Hispanic woman popped her head into the room. When she saw Raina, she asked, "Housekeeping?"

Raina nodded. "Go ahead. There's no need to make the bed." She never understood the logic of why someone needed to make the bed in the morning only to return to it at night.

She grabbed her purse and decided to clean it out while she waited for her grandma. She tossed out meal receipts, inkless pens, and half-eaten granola bars she meant to save for later.

"Excuse me?" The maid held out a USB memory stick. "This yours?"

Raina frowned. "Where did you find this?" She didn't recognize the memory stick, but it could belong to Matthew.

The maid pointed at the entertainment unit. "I found it..." She made a dusting motion with her hand.

Raina glanced at the dresser drawer. Could the USB stick belong to Claire? Her pulse jumped at the thought. There was still a chance the memory stick had belonged to a previous guest. She slipped the memory stick into her purse. "Thank you."

The maid returned to the bathroom and continued cleaning.

Raina should probably leave the maid alone, but there weren't many opportunities to talk to the staff without a crowd waiting for their turn. She followed the maid to the bathroom and leaned casually against the doorframe.

"I hate to bother you, but I sent my clothes down for laundry service yesterday, and I haven't gotten them back yet," Raina said. "Usually the service is very prompt with returning my clothes the next morning. Do you know what's going on down there?"

The maid froze, and her grip tightened on the toilet brush until white knuckles stood out in her hand.

From the woman's body language, Raina knew the maid had a visceral reaction to the question. She wondered if gossip exaggerated the horror downstairs. "Are you okay?" she asked softly.

The maid stood up from the toilet and held the brush in front of her, pointing it at Raina. "No laundry room." As she spoke, she shook her hands, and droplets of liquid from the toilet brush scattered in front of her.

Raina jumped back but felt wet spots on her thighs. She didn't stop to look at her pants. Her heart kicked up a notch at the unusual confrontation, but no one could win a fight with a toilet brush.

"I told the *policía* everything. I not know how lady got in bag," the maid said. Her Spanish accent grew stronger with each sentence.

Raina continued to back away until the back of her thigh hit the corner of the sofa. "I'm going to wait for my grandma outside." She opened the door, stepped out into the hallway, and closed it behind her.

She glanced down at her pants. There were still several wet spots on the fabric. Fantastic. Now she could walk around smelling like a mountain spring.

A door clicked open. Raina glanced up to see Po Po stepping into in the hallway from her room.

"Rainy, you're early. I thought we synchronized our watches," Po Po said with disappointment.

"I just got attacked by a maid brandishing a toilet brush," Raina said. She explained what happened in her room. "I have a feeling she discovered the body. It's too bad she has to come to work today. She could probably use a day at home."

"She probably needs the pay. I don't see this place giving her a mental health day. Do you want me to go in there and talk to her?"

"I don't know. She seems mighty upset."

Po Po rolled her neck and cracked her knuckles. "Let me work my magic. I'm going in. Don't worry, honey. I got this."

Raina suppressed a smile at the determined look on her grandma's face. If Po Po wanted toilet water flung at her face, who was Raina to stop her? "Can I use your laptop?" Her grandma always traveled with her laptop. Sometimes Raina wondered what kind of business Po Po conducted while on the go.

Po Po nodded. "It's on my bed."

Raina opened the door to her room and held it open. Po Po disappeared into the suite. Raina used the spare key card and entered her grandma's suite, calling out, "Maggie, it's me. Just borrowing Po Po's computer."

Maggie waved in greeting and returned to her conversation on her cell phone. Raina paused, studying the turned shoulder and cupped hands around the phone. It was obvious Maggie didn't want eavesdroppers. While Matthew's grandma was calmer than Po Po, they were best friends for a reason. Raina had a feeling the whispered conversation might come back to bite her in the rear.

Raina went into the bedroom, dismissing the random thought. She didn't have time to worry about Maggie at the moment. She grabbed Po Po's laptop from the bed, entered the password, and inserted the USB stick.

She held her breath, hoping the drive wouldn't automatically run a program. She would hate to download a virus onto her grandma's laptop, although Po Po had an entire club of high schoolers who could remove the virus for pizza and energy drinks.

Raina clicked on the USB drive and a screen popped up asking for a password. She tried several common passwords. No dice. She pulled out the USB stick and powered down the laptop. It looked like they might need the high school students and their hacking skills after all.

As she passed the living room, she called out, "I'm leaving."

Maggie was no longer on the phone and returned to her knitting. "Have fun sleuthing."

Raina paused again. Something in Maggie's voice seemed off. "Is everything okay? I hope you're not upset that we keep leaving you in the room."

"Everything is peachy." Maggie made a shooing motion with her hands. "Now get out of here. You're interrupting my show."

Raina grabbed the guitar next to the door and left the suite, feeling unsatisfied. Was Maggie acting strangely because she had heard from Matthew? But why would Matthew only call his grandma? She pulled out her cell phone, and there was a voicemail message. It was from an unfamiliar number in Las Vegas. She listened to the message. It was from Hendricks.

"Miss Sun, please call me back. Willie said you wanted to review the surveillance video outside of your room. I checked out the video this morning..." His voice trailed off, and there was a long pause. "We need to talk before I turn this over to the police."

Raina's heart sank. Hendricks must have seen Raina chasing Claire out of her room. This was going to make her look bad. She hoped Claire didn't die when Raina was alone and couldn't produce an alibi.

"WHAT'S GOING ON? Cat got your tongue?" Po Po asked, stepping out into the hallway and closing the door behind her. She glanced at her smartwatch. "Let's walk and chat. We'll be late for the guitar seminar."

Raina trailed off after her grandma, holding onto the guitar case. It was big and bulky enough that holding it by the handle made her feel lopsided, but she also could not hold it in front of her with two hands. Lugging this thing around for more than a short trip downstairs could be a pain.

"I think trouble just found me." Raina told her grandma the message from Hendricks.

Po Po stabbed the call button for the elevator, poking it several times as if this would make the elevator come faster. "Do you want to split up?"

Raina hesitated. She would love to split up and get more done. She didn't want to wait too long because Hendricks might get antsy and call the police. But neither did she want her grandma to interview Brian Anderson by herself. As much as she loved Po Po, her grandma was a loose cannon. She would think nothing of accusing Brian Anderson of being a murderer in front of everyone and browbeating him into a confession.

"Here's the plan," Raina said. "You go ahead to the guitar seminar and follow Brian around incognito. I'll talk to Hendricks, and I'll try to make it back before the seminar ends. But if I don't, you'll have him under surveillance until I show up. Do not approach the mark without me. You'll need backup in case everything goes up in flames."

Po Po saluted. "I got your back, Sherlock."

Raina smiled inwardly. She had used all the right words— incognito, surveillance, mark, and flames—so her grandma thought she was on a spy mission. This should keep Po Po from approaching Brian Anderson until Raina got back.

The elevator came, and they got into the empty car.

"Did you get any information from the maid?" Raina asked.

"The maid came in at seven o'clock to start her shift. After putting her purse in the locker, she went upstairs with the other maids to start their housekeeping duties. When she came back downstairs to the laundry room at about eight thirty there were already several bags of laundry waiting for her," Po Po said.

"Where did the laundry come from?"

"The maids drop them off when they fill up their linen bag. It was our maid's turn to do the laundry this week. She loaded up the two machines. And then another group of maids came down to drop off their full bags. She went with them across the hall to the storage room. When the maids went back upstairs, she started her second load of laundry. And that's when she discovered the body."

"What time did she start the second load?" Raina said.

"She doesn't know."

Raina frowned. "A load of laundry wouldn't take more than thirty-five or forty minutes in the industrial machines downstairs. Even if you add in gabbing time with the other women, the maid probably started the second load about an hour after she came downstairs."

They stepped out of the elevator and headed toward the Sunset Room. The casino floor was crowded with rock star impersonators mingling with the regular folks. If only Raina had more time to appreciate the spectacle.

"So nine thirty-ish?" Po Po asked.

"The killer probably dumped Claire's body in the laundry room sometime between seven fifteen-ish and nine thirty am."

Po Po's eyes widened. "We didn't go downstairs for breakfast until nine."

"And I was seen chasing her a few hours before." Raina swallowed uneasily. She had no alibi.

"You're overthinking this. You have no motive for killing Claire. The police could not seriously consider you a suspect."

Raina wasn't so sure. What if instead of doing a slapdash investigation, the police looked for a scapegoat? A young out-of-towner scraping by on two part-time jobs. Yeah, she would make the perfect scapegoat.

"I'm not worried about being a murder suspect," she lied. "I'm worried about the cost of the lodging if we can't leave town. It must cost Matthew a fortune for the two suites."

"Let him worry about that. It's his fault we are here

without a groom. But in the meantime, we have something to occupy our time. This is better than sitting around and picking our bellybutton lint."

Raina smiled at the comment. Trust her grandma to think a murder investigation would fight off boredom.

"Did you get what you needed from my laptop?" Po Po asked.

Raina shook her head. "The maid found a USB drive by the entertainment unit where Claire Boucher was snooping around. But there's a password lock on it, and I don't know the password."

"Do you want me to overnight it to one of my Science Ninjas kids? They can make a copy and get the original back to us in a couple of days. They'll crack the password for pizza and Red Bull. I might have to throw in a gift card to GameStop to turn up the heat on the competition among the kids.

Raina bit her lower lip. The USB memory stick could be evidence, or it might be nothing. And given what she knew of city government's limited resources, they probably wouldn't have anyone on staff who could hack the password protection software within a reasonable time frame, if at all.

Besides, if one of the high school kids could open the files and get the evidence out, then they would be helping the police. And since there were already several sets of handprints on the USB drive, it probably didn't matter if they got a couple more on it.

"Let's do it," Raina said.

Po Po gave her a thumbs up. "You got it, boss."

By this time, they were outside the Sunset Room. Raina handed Po Po the guitar. "Remember, you're only here to observe. Do not engage the mark. Have fun, and I will see you later."

6

────

A BEARDED MAN

Raina returned to the casino floor and asked the nearest server in the skimpy outfit where she could find the security office. She was directed to a room next to the elevator on the second floor. As she made her way to Hendricks's office, she considered her options.

She could beg him not to turn over the video clips to the police. Even though her action was suspicious, chasing Claire to the casino floor wasn't incriminating, especially when Claire snuck into Raina's suite in the first place. But it probably wasn't a good idea to get on the police's radar with Matthew working on a secret assignment.

Besides, even if she groveled, Hendricks would still release the videos. Raina had a feeling she had offended Hendricks by asking about Matthew's contract work with the hotel-casino. At the time she had believed her fiancé's cover story, but Hendricks might take her questioning as encroaching on his territory. It would be much cheaper to hire goons for monitoring the video feeds than to bring in a contractor for upgrades. Management might figure out there was no need for a head of security.

Raina knocked on the door with a metal plaque that said "Security" on it. She glanced up to see a camera pointing at her. With all these cameras and their blinking red lights in the hotel-casino, one of them should have recorded who entered the laundry room with a bloodstained bag.

Or maybe some cameras with the blinking red lights were fakes. Many homeowners used fake cameras outside their homes to fool would-be burglars, and they had been shown to prevent breakins. It was much cheaper than continuous monitoring for the rare times when there was a crime.

The casino floor, the shopping area, and exits had cameras behind smoke half domes on the ceilings. Those were probably continuously monitored. However, the cameras with the blinking red lights seemed to be in the hallways of the guest rooms. She couldn't remember if they were by the elevators.

A pregnant woman opened the door and gestured for Raina to come in. The room was dimly lit, and there were banks of monitors along one wall. In front of the monitors, a man ate his breakfast burrito at the long counter with a central console that had enough buttons, dials, and switches to satisfy a child on the playground. The pregnant woman closed the door and returned to her seat at the counter and the movie playing on her smartphone.

Raina blinked. The hotel-casino was a block behind the Strip, but she still expected security to be more professional. At the corner office—it was more like a broom closet—Hendricks waited with crossed arms. Once Raina stepped into his domain, he closed the door. In contrast to the dimly lit room outside, the fluorescent lights overhead were unnaturally bright and reminded her of an interrogation room.

After they sat down, Hendricks leaned back on his thinly padded office chair and steepled his hands on his chest. There was just enough room for Raina to squeeze into the metal folding chair in front of the battered oak desk. A taller person would bang her knees on the desk each time she shifted. He studied Raina for a long moment.

Raina raised an eyebrow. Was she supposed to be intimidated, especially after the amateur act in the command center? She sat back and crossed her arms, waiting for him to speak first.

Hendricks must have realized that she wasn't admitting to anything. He swiveled his computer monitor until Raina could see the screen. He tapped on his keyboard. "Can you explain this?"

The display showed two views, one for each of the cameras in the service hall. In one view, a tall, muscular Asian man stepped through the double swinging doors from the casino floor. The man wore a baseball cap and had a full beard.

Raina bit the inside of her cheek to stop from gasping out loud. It was Matthew. Even the grainy black-and-white picture quality couldn't hide the way her fiancé moved and held himself as if ready for trouble.

In the other view, the service elevator opened, and Claire Boucher stepped out and waited for him outside the laundry room door. Her face looked pinched, and her hands were tucked underneath her armpits like they were cold. She still wore her orange lanyard name tag, but she seemed to have lost her half-moon reading glasses. She shifted from foot to foot while waiting for Matthew and kept glancing at the side door as if expecting someone.

Raina folded her shaking hands on her lap, hiding them from Hendricks's view. So she had been right—Matthew was on a secret assignment. But she would have never guessed that he would have a rendezvous with the convention organizer. She silently prayed that Claire was killed when Matthew was miles away.

On the screen, Matthew approached Claire, and they disappeared inside the laundry room and closed the door. Ten minutes later, Matthew came out. The full beard hid the expression on his face, but the furrow between his brows told Raina that he wasn't happy with the meeting. He exited through the side door.

Hendricks paused the video clip. "Do you know this man?"

Raina dragged her attention from the screen and

focused on the head of security. Even though a voice was screaming inside her head, she was outwardly calm. Anything less could ruin Matthew's assignment. Whatever trouble he was in, he only needed time to clear up the misunderstanding. And she was more than willing to help buy him time.

"No," Raina said through numb lips. "I don't recognize him."

Hendricks made a sound that could have been a growl. His fingers stabbed at the keyboard, and the service hall disappeared from the monitor. A new video clip replaced it. On the screen, Raina stood next to Matthew, checking in at the lobby of the hotel-casino a few days ago. The grandmas stood behind them and guarded their luggage.

"Do you know this man?" Hendricks asked. There was steel in his voice.

Raina studied the man with the square head and square body. His beefy form spilled out from the cheap office chair. Even though the command center and the security guards outside were a joke, Hendricks looked like a man who knew how to dig a hole in the desert sand. Okay, she might be slightly intimidated now.

"That's my fiancé. We were checking in," she said, hoping she sounded confused. Sometimes the bimbolina act worked with intimidating men. If Hendricks underestimated her intelligence, she might leave with nothing worse than a warning.

"Aha! So you do know the laundry room killer." There was a hint of satisfaction in his too bright eyes.

She blinked. Did he dub the murderer with a nickname? The hooded expression he had shown at the time of the body's discovery might have been an act to hide his lack of competence. "Who's the killer? The maid?"

Hendricks placed both hands on the metal desk and leaned forward. "Your fiancé."

Raina's heart sped up. She didn't know if Hendricks was guessing or if he had concrete evidence pointing to Matthew. "The man with the beard? But he's not my fiancé."

"It's the same person," Hendricks said through gritted teeth. "The beard is a fake." He tapped on his keyboard again and returned to the service hall and zoomed in on Matthew's face.

Raina studied the image. It was the first glimpse she had seen of him in over three days. Her fingers twitched as if wanting to touch the screen. "How do you know the facial hair is fake? I can't tell from the picture quality."

"Because your fiancé couldn't have grown a full beard in a few days."

"The same could be said for any man. I know you think all Asians look alike, but that man is not my fiancé." Raina grimaced inwardly. Throwing down the race card was a low blow, but it might get Hendricks to back off.

Hendricks raised an eyebrow. "Where is your fiancé now, Miss Sun?"

"He's working."

"Where is he working?"

"As I told you before, he's doing a security upgrade. I thought it was for this hotel because we're staying here, but he might be working for one of the bigger hotels on the Strip." There. Maybe Hendricks could relax now that his job wasn't at stake. She didn't think Matthew was working for a hotel at all.

"I plan to turn over these videos to the police."

Raina ignored the bait. She wasn't groveling over something that was the normal protocol for a murder investigation. "Probably a good idea. Maybe they'll have someone on the force who can tell Asians apart."

"You could get thrown in jail as an accessory," he said in a patronizing tone. "You wouldn't want to be in there with the drunks and the prostitutes. Vegas isn't a nice town for a nice girl like you."

"Are you threatening me?" Raina asked, leaning forward in her seat. "My uncle is one of the highest-paid criminal defense lawyers in San Francisco. And his son clerks for the Supreme Court. Do I need to make a phone call?"

Her extended family was filled with professionals with multiple letters after their names and prosperous entrepreneurs. The Sun branch of the family wasn't as prestigious, but being Chinese, the family would be more than willing to step in and help the "poor relation." And she would have to be behind bars with no release in sight before she would call for their help, but Hendricks didn't know this.

Hendricks swallowed. "That's for the police to decide. My job is to report criminal activity."

Raina smiled inwardly. She had made her point, and there was no need to gloat. Time to see if she could squeeze information from the security team. "Can we watch this video clip again? I want to see what happens after the maid put in the laundry. At this point, she didn't seem to discover the body yet."

He complied and played the video.

A few minutes later, Raina said, "The killer is one of the maids."

Hendricks shook his head. "We run background checks on all our employees. None of the women has a history of violence."

Raina didn't want to argue. In situations like murder, the killer was a regular person who snapped when pushed to her limit. "Replay the video, and I'll show you what I see."

Hendricks replayed the video.

A maid came out of the service elevator and went inside the laundry room. It might have been the woman who cleaned Raina's room earlier, but she couldn't tell from the picture quality. Through the open doorway, Raina could see the maid tossing laundry into the industrial washing machines. She glanced at the time stamp at the corner of the screen. 8:25 AM. The first load of laundry.

After the laundry maid started the load, four maids got off the service elevator and went inside the laundry room with full linen bags hanging off their carts. A few minutes later, all five of them came out, two of them pushing the carts, and crossed the service hall.

"Pause here," Raina said.

Hendricks tapped on the keyboard.

Raina pointed at the screen. "Four maids dropped off dirty linen bags in the laundry room. Two for each cart. Are the maids usually paired up?"

Hendricks shrugged. "I'll have to ask the head housekeeper. I don't know their routine."

"Here we have five maids. The one inside the laundry room joined her co-workers. Notice how all of them are chatting and smiling. They appear to be friends."

"Yes, I can see this," Hendricks said with a hint of sarcasm. "What is your point?"

Raina ignored his tone. She couldn't understand why he didn't see what she saw. "Just watch. Please hit play again."

He sighed and tapped on the keyboard.

The maids went inside the storage room. They were inside for a good fifteen minutes. Then four maids went into the service elevator with their carts.

"That's four of them leaving the scene," Raina said.

Hendricks grunted in acknowledgment.

On the screen, the last maid returned to the laundry room. A few minutes later, she stumbled into the service hall with wide eyes and fear written across her face. She ran down to the double swinging doors toward the casino floor.

"That's maid number five," Raina said.

Hendricks reached for the keyboard.

"Wait," Raina said. "Let's see what happens next."

The video showed an empty hall. The seconds dragged by.

"What are we waiting for?" Hendricks finally asked.

At this moment, a shadow moved in the laundry room.

Raina pointed at it. "There!"

A sixth maid came out of the laundry room. She kept her head tucked close to her neck. The oversized glasses and big hair hid her face. She strolled purposefully toward the double swinging doors.

Before she could go through, a man came in. He said something to her, and she pointed toward the laundry room. As he ran down the service hall, she disappeared through the double doors.

"Where did she come from?" Hendricks asked. The astonishment on his face could have been comedic.

"I think she had been hiding inside the laundry room all this time. Who was the man that spoke to her?"

"He's one of the pit bosses."

"Maybe he could identify her," Raina said.

Hendricks tapped on his keyboard and replayed the entire scene again. When he got to the part where the sixth maid came out of the laundry room, he paused and zoomed in on the woman's face.

"She could be anybody. The picture quality is too grainy. And I don't think the pit boss paid enough attention to pick out the killer maid from a lineup."

"What about the cameras on the casino floor?" Raina asked.

Hendricks cycled through multiple camera feeds, looking for the killer maid. "One camera caught her stepping onto the casino floor, but then she disappeared into the crowd." He paused the video feed to show the wraparound line waiting for the buffet in front of the service hall entrance.

Raina shook her head. "She didn't disappear, but she probably transformed her appearance so we can't find her. She could have taken off her glasses, tucked her hair into a ponytail or a bun. The uniform is a black T-shirt and black pants. Underneath it, she could have on a different color shirt. As she walked through the crowd, she could've taken off her shirt. No one would have looked twice or remarked on her actions."

Hendricks gave Raina a sharp look. "You're watching too many spy movies. This kind of stuff doesn't happen in real life."

Raina ignored his comment. "But when did the killer maid go into the laundry room? Can we look at an earlier time? Maybe we can catch her sneaking in."

Hendricks tapped on his keyboard, bringing up the video feed in the service hall at 7 AM. The video showed several women pushing carts out of the storage room and onto the service elevator. After the women headed upstairs, there was no activity.

With over two thousand rooms, there must be over one hundred maids on the housekeeping staff. Raina counted the fifteen carts. This meant thirty maids regularly used the service elevator in this wing of the building.

Hendricks sped the video feed forward until the side door opened. On the monitor, a maid came into the service hall and disappeared into the laundry room.

Raina glanced at the time stamp. 7:35 AM. "The killer maid timed it perfectly. How did she know when the real maids would clear the area? Is there a posted schedule?"

Hendricks shrugged. "I'm assuming they do their morning tailgate meeting like we do. So they share info for the first fifteen minutes of their shift. And the service elevator can only fit four carts at a time, so it takes a few minutes to get everyone upstairs."

Raina considered his words. Several rooms in this wing of the building looked out to the loading dock area. An observant person could figure out when the maids came in for their shift based on the activity in the parking lot.

A conversation with one of the maids could probably give the killer maid enough information to figure out there would be a thirty- to forty-minute gap where the service hall would be empty in the morning.

And there was an exit for a quick getaway. It might be why Matthew and Claire decided to meet here. But how did the killer maid know the rendezvous would take place in the laundry room?

"What's next? Will you talk to housekeeping?" Raina asked.

"I plan to talk to the police about my discovery. You should get back to enjoying your vacation," Hendricks said.

Raina bristled inwardly at the dismissal in his voice. If this was how he wanted to play the game, she was happy to comply. "So if I find out anything else, I guess you wouldn't want to know."

"It is your civic duty to help the authorities with an investigation," he said.

Raina waited until she left the command center before rolling her eyes. During the walk toward the elevator, she reviewed what she had learned. Whoever killed Claire Boucher had to be someone close to the victim. After all, how did the killer maid find out about the laundry room rendezvous?

7

ANOTHER ENGAGEMENT

Raina got as far as the giant slot machine that promised one winner a brand new Mustang when her cell phone buzzed. It was a text message from her grandma.

SOS. COME UP TO MY ROOM LICKETY-QUICK.

Raina dialed her grandma's cell phone, but it went straight to voice mail. She stared at her phone, debating if the message was urgent or just Po Po urgent. Sometimes her grandma's sense of urgency had a way of complicating things.

She had less than five minutes to get to the convention room where the guitar seminar was held. If she missed this opportunity, she might not be able to track down Brian Anderson again.

What was her grandma doing in her room in the first place? Po Po's assignment was to keep an eye on the mark. Her grandma wouldn't have abandoned her post unless something happened to Maggie. After all, the family came first.

Raina sighed and turned around. She trotted toward the elevator. Somebody better be bleeding upstairs. If the two ladies were just bickering like children...

She used the spare key card and opened the door to the grandma suite. Po Po sat on the reading chair, arms folded across her chest, and a frown on her face. Sitting across from her were Maggie and Frank Small on the sofa. All three faces glanced at the door expectantly. Even Poe, the service dog, lifted his head from his position at Maggie's feet to look at the doorway.

Raina shifted her gaze from face to face, and a sense of uneasiness settled into her stomach. What was Frank doing here?

The retired ex-military man was part of her grandma's Posse Club at the senior center at home. He was still over six feet tall and in good shape thanks to tennis. His dark brown skin contrasted with his white hair. He hunched on the sofa as if trying to make himself as small as possible between the two tiny Chinese women.

Normally, the three of them were the best of friends and had an easy jovial air about them. Today, all three of them were rigid and sat with enough space between them as if they were strangers. Whatever was happening here, Raina had a feeling she was called in to referee. Great.

"What's going on here?" Raina asked. Might as well get this over with.

Po Po jerked a thumb at the couple on the sofa. "Big and Tiny are getting married. They're going to have a Las Vegas shotgun wedding."

Raina's jaw dropped. Big and Tiny were Frank's and Maggie's code names when the Posse Club was in an active mission. She had thought the two paired off because the ex-military man was looking out for the half-blind lady.

She never suspected the two of them were romantically involved. And apparently, neither did her grandma. Was there a hint of jealousy in her grandma's voice? And how would Matthew react to the news?

Maggie gazed at Raina with a hopeful expression. Her insecurity was written all over her face, and she wanted Raina on her side.

Frank had a mulish expression on his face. His jaw tightened. He was also waiting for Raina to say something.

And Po Po was frowning at Raina like she was already a traitor.

Raina gave all three of them a beaming smile. "Congratulations. I am so happy for the two of you."

And she was happy for them. After all, it wasn't often two people found another chance at a romance, especially in their golden years. She didn't know why her grandma wasn't happy with the situation, but this wasn't the time for a discussion.

"But I got to go," Raina said, opening the door

again. "I need to catch one of the murder suspects before he takes off."

"You're in another murder investigation again?" Frank asked, brightening up. "Anything I can do to help?"

"Po Po will fill you in. She's great at organizing everyone. I got to go." Raina left the suite and closed the door behind her with a sigh of relief. Talk about complications.

As she trotted toward the elevator, once again, Raina couldn't help but hear the echo of laughter from her ancestors. Or maybe they were the Louie ancestors. Why did Maggie have to get engaged on Raina's watch? Couldn't she have waited until her grandson returned and then announced the news?

Raina got into the elevator and punched the button for the first floor. Maybe Maggie didn't wait because she wanted Raina to pave the way before she spoke to Matthew. Geez... another family expectation.

Matthew should be mature enough to be happy for his grandma, but Raina had a feeling he might react worse than Po Po. Maggie was the only family he had, and now he would have to share her affections.

And it wouldn't matter to him that he was about to start a family of his own with Raina. She hoped she was overthinking this, but pigs didn't fly, and her man was an overprotective bear when it came to his family. He might even be silly enough to think Frank would use his grandma as a nursemaid.

THE GUITAR SEMINAR was long over by the time Raina made her way to the convention area. The Sunset Room was half empty with attendees coming and going. She scanned the crowd, looking for a bad toupee and sideburns. No dice. If she had hair like Brian Anderson, she would put on a wig too. Since she didn't know what he looked like in costume, scanning the crowd was no help. She didn't know him well enough to pick him out quickly with a change to his hair color and style.

Wait a minute. Brian Anderson lost his name badge. What she should look for was somebody with a handwritten name badge like the one she wore around her neck. She lowered her gaze to chest level, drifting through the crowd and scanning their badges. It was a lucky thing she was obviously female even in costume because staring at everyone's chest earned her some funny looks.

There! In the corner was a man with a handwritten badge talking to Willie Machado. The tawny blonde general manager towered over the slight man in her three-inch stiletto pumps. Brian stood behind his guitar case, his hands resting on top of the case as if warding off an attack.

Raina circled the room, edging closer and closer to Brian and Willie until she sat down behind them in one of the chairs. She pulled out the program from her purse and pretended to study it intently with a pen in her hand.

Up close, Brian looked nothing like the mob leader confronting Claire two days ago. Without anger burning through his eyes, the pale blue was overshadowed by the red veins.

"Are you sure we have to tell the attendees about it?" Brian said. He took off his jet-black wig and wiped the sweat off his forehead.

Willie placed her hand on her hip. She wore a red pantsuit that normally would have made her a beacon in any crowd but was eclipsed by the colors, crystals, and sequins in this one. "Yes, you do. And I also need you to give me a list of people who might want Claire Boucher dead."

The gravelly voice sent a shiver down Raina's back.

"I can't do this. It would be hearsay. I didn't witness anything," Brian said.

Raina rolled her eyes. Of course, he couldn't give her a suspect list. He would be at the top of it. And as the general manager, why would she investigate Claire's death in the first place? Didn't she have a business to run?

Through the doorway, Raina caught sight of a tall man in a white blazer and jeans talking to a uniformed police officer in the hallway. She ducked her head and held the program close to her face. He strolled in and made a beeline for Brian and Willie.

Raina had been dismissed before she had a chance to speak with Detective Lamar Stafford at the crime scene, but she could recognize him anywhere. He was a few years older than Matthew. His skin was a lighter shade than Frank Small, not exactly café au lait, but more of a brown sugar.

"Brian Anderson?" Detective Stafford spoke with an accent that was not quite British or Australian. "Detective Lamar Stafford of the LVPD. Can I speak to you for a moment?"

Raina snuck a glance at the detective, ducked her head again, and circled something on her program. His hazel eyes were too alert for Raina's comfort. He would want to talk to Matthew after watching the video feed.

Brian shifted. "What can I help you with, Detective?"

"Maybe we should go someplace more private. It is about Claire Boucher."

"Will this take more than five minutes? I am moderating the panel." Brian gestured toward the table at the front of the room and the five people sitting behind it.

"Can we talk afterward?" Detective Stafford asked.

Brian nodded. "The panel is scheduled for ninety minutes."

"I'll wait for you outside in the hallway. Willie, please pencil me in for this afternoon. Is two o'clock good?"

Willie nodded, spun on her heels, and marched out of the room.

Raina resisted the urge to stroke her chin. Interesting. The general manager seemed a little too antagonistic toward Detective Stafford. Was there some history between the two of them?

"In the meantime, I would like to ask Miss Sun a few questions," Detective Stafford said.

Raina froze. How did he know? She snuck a peek up from underneath her lashes to find his hazel eyes looking down at her. Heat rose to her face. So busted.

She folded the program and tucked it back into her purse. She got up and strode out of the Sunset Room. There was no point in arguing or justifying her snooping. And since Detective Stafford wanted to speak to her, he would follow her out.

He caught up with her in the hallway by the bench facing the Sunset Room. Before she could sit down for a comfortable chat, he said, "I heard you like iced coffee. Let's go grab one at the coffee shop."

Raina blinked. Was he hitting on her? Or was he intentionally throwing her off, pretending like they were on friendly terms so he could spin circles around her with his questions? Either way, this was most irregular and highly unprofessional. She brushed a strand of hair off her face, making sure that the light caught the ring on her finger.

Detective Stafford didn't even glance at her hand.

So he wasn't interested in Raina romantically. Interesting. Did he think she might have information that he didn't have? "Sure."

They strode to the café in silence, side-by-side, like they could be old friends who didn't need to talk to fill the space between them. During this time Raina's mind raced through a hundred different scenarios. This was new territory for her. Usually, the detectives either told her to stay out of police business, asked her for help, or dismissed her as a nuisance. This was something else entirely.

Maybe his suggestion to grab a coffee had nothing to do with the case and everything to do with his need for caffeine. After all, he probably stayed up all night reviewing the videos. The hotel-casino must want him to wrap up the investigation as soon as possible. And with this kind of money, they undoubtedly put the squeeze on the police department, and the brown stuff trickled down onto him.

The café was a Starbucks clone, except for the smoke. The ventilation system wasn't strong enough to remove the slight haze in the air. Customers dangled a cigarette in one hand while holding on to a disposable coffee cup in the other. Raina cleared her throat, but it didn't remove the grit from the back of her throat.

They ordered coffee—his was black, and hers was an iced caramel macchiato—and paid for them separately. They found two black leather reading chairs in a corner. Raina had to sit sideways, so she didn't have to touch his knees.

Detective Stafford waited until Raina took a sip of coffee. "Tell me what happened yesterday."

Raina took another slow sip of coffee, hoping to buy her some time. Should she mention her concern about Matthew? Maybe she should play it by ear. See how he questioned her and whether he was a good cop.

She told him about finding Claire in her suite in the morning and talking to Willie. "We went downstairs, hoping to run into the security guy." This wasn't exactly a lie. They were supposed to meet with Hendricks to go over the video feed as directed by Willie. Things just got sidetracked by the discovery of the body.

Detective Stafford frowned. "This is the first time I heard about the victim being in your room. Do you know why she was there?"

Raina shook her head.

"Hendricks showed me the video surveillance of the hotel-casino the last twenty-four hours before Claire's death. I didn't see her in the hallway outside your suite."

"That's because it is being"—she made air quotes with her fingers—"recorded with the cameras with the blinking red lights. Those are fake."

Detective Stafford gave her a doubtful look. "How did you come to this conclusion?"

Raina explained her theory about the cameras with the blinking red lights and the cameras hidden behind smoky half domes. She pointed at the blinking red light at the back wall. "Fake. If you go ask Hendricks there's no video footage of the café."

He studied the camera for a long moment.

"With Big Brother watching, you'll want to be on

your best behavior," she said. "No butt scratching or underwear adjusting."

"I learn something new every day," he said without a hint of sarcasm.

Detective Stafford hadn't pulled out a notebook to write down anything she had said. Neither did he pretend to consult a notebook to circle back to a point.

"Shouldn't you write something down?" she asked.

He tapped the side of his head. "It's all in here. I have a photographic memory. It's my superpower. Kind of like Sherlock Holmes."

She didn't reply. Or maybe this was a charade like the blinking red lights?

He sipped his coffee and studied her as if waiting to see if she would babble to fill in the silence.

She sipped her coffee and returned his stare. Better to keep silent unless he asked a direct question.

"Where is your fiancé, Miss Sun?" he asked.

8

OLD BUDDIES

Raina choked, and iced coffee squirted out of her nose. She grabbed a napkin and covered the lower half of her face while she continued to cough.

"Are you okay?" Detective Stafford asked.

"Wrong pipe," Raina wheezed.

She squeezed her eyes shut, hoping to give herself a moment to think. From the way Detective Stafford asked the question, he had seen the video of Matthew leaving the laundry room. And he made the same assumption as Hendricks that the man with the base-ball cap and beard was her fiancé.

She couldn't play the race card again, at least not with a straight face to another minority. If only she could unburden her worries about Matthew to some-one. But she couldn't risk it. Not if it meant potentially compromising her fiancé.

Raina told him the same lie that she had told

Hendricks. "Matthew has to be in one of the hotels. He has a habit of turning off his cell phone when he's in the middle of his work. He's very focused. And he believed that our species had survived generations without cell phones attached to their hips, so he's not planning to start now." She snapped her mouth shut. She was starting to babble.

"This doesn't sound like the Elliot Matthew Louie that I knew back in our old Marine days. He was supposed to look me up when he was in town, but the last time I heard from him was a text message saying he had to disappear for a while," Detective Stafford said.

Raina stiffened, and the pleasant smile froze on her face. If Matthew had meant to look up his old buddy, he would have told her.

Detective Stafford pulled out his cell phone and opened the text app.

Raina gave the phone a perfunctory glance. There was a message from a "Matthew," but it might not be her Matthew. Short of tapping on his phone to check the actual number, she still hadn't seen any proof the two men were old buddies. And old buddies didn't translate to friends now. Boy, was she getting cynical or what.

"So how did you meet Matthew?" Raina asked.

Detective Stafford spun a tale about meeting in the desert of Afghanistan. Apparently, Matthew had saved his bacon when a pipe bomb went off on them during a routine patrol. The story sounded plausible.

However, Raina didn't think Matthew spent time doing routine patrol. He had specialized in geographic information systems, and his unit worked mostly with drones and mapping the data on GIS for strategic deployment.

When the detective finished his story, Raina asked, "Did he tell you what he was doing in Las Vegas?"

Detective Stafford shook his head. "He didn't say. But when I saw your name in the case file, I knew he would want me to check on you, to make sure you and your grandma were okay."

The detective was a charming and urbane man, but he was also a liar. And this made Raina question his motive. She didn't think he was the murderer, but he might have a personal stake in the case. He tried just a little too hard to gain her trust by revealing a friendship with Matthew that was unlikely to exist.

"It's a good thing his grandma wasn't with us. She is a feisty one," Raina said, testing his knowledge on the Louie family. Maggie Louie was the more docile grandma, but he didn't know this.

"I thought she was a typical granny who liked to knit countless scarves. She used to feed me pork buns when I went home with Matthew for the holidays."

Ah-ha! Raina finally got the evidence he was a liar. Maggie always spent the holidays with Po Po and her extended family. And Matthew showed up when he was on the same coast. If the detective had visited the Louies for any holiday, he would have shown up at one of these family gatherings. What did he hope to gain by pretending to be a family friend?

"Are you sure Claire Boucher didn't take anything from your room? Or maybe she hid something in there?" Detective Stafford asked casually.

Raina shook her head. "Not a thing. I want to know how she got the key card to my room."

"She didn't need a key card. The locks are easy enough to pick."

Raina sat back and thought about his words. Claire had moved in the predawn light with the practiced ease of a cat burglar. At least that was Raina's impression upon waking. Maybe Claire did have training on how to pick a lock.

"Where do we go from here?" Raina asked.

"What you mean? Won't Matthew turn up soon?"

"I'm talking about the murder investigation. Will you question Brian Anderson soon?"

Detective Stafford glanced at the Fitbit on his wrist. "In about ten minutes."

The detective started asking Raina some uncomfortable questions about Matthew and his relationship with the victim. Before Raina could make something up, escape came in the form of her grandma.

"What's up, Sherlock?" said a familiar voice nearby.

Raina spun around to see her grandma, sitting next to them, with a floppy hat and large Jackie O sunglasses. She had changed into a skimpy sundress and cardigan. She wore a cone bra on the outside like Madonna in the eighties. Raina didn't recall seeing such an outrageous outfit when she sat down, but her grandma could have snuck in later.

Po Po took off her glasses and batted false long lashes at the detective. Her mouth curved into a slow smile. "Well, hello, young man. You can call me Bonnie." She growled and inched closer.

Detective Stafford got a deer in headlights look. "Um, hello?"

Raina bit the inside of her cheek to keep from giggling like a child.

This was all the invitation Po Po needed. She got up and sat on the arm of his reading chair, bracing one hand on the backrest so that her cone-shaped boobs were in his face. "Is it my time to answer questions, Detective?" she said in a low sultry voice. "I think my daughter has hogged you long enough."

"I thought Raina was your granddaughter," he said, edging away.

Raina couldn't tell if he was blushing, but he certainly looked like he wanted the earth to swallow him whole.

"Raina's my daughter. It's the sun damage. I keep telling her to use sunblock, or it'll age her. But does she listen to her dear mommy? Of course not. Look at her now."

Raina snickered. Great. Her grandma had lost two decades since the last time they spoke, and apparently, Raina had gained them.

Po Po brushed the side of his neck with a finger.

"Don't let the white hair fool you. I still have a lot of bounce where it counts.

Detective Stafford jerked as if her grandma had stabbed him. His coffee squirted out of the cup and splashed across his lap, staining his white blazer and pale blue jeans.

"Oh, let me help you with that," Po Po said, pulling napkins from her cone bra to dab at his groin. Her cones almost took out his eyes.

Detective Stafford jumped up. "Call me if you hear from Matthew," he said to Raina. He bolted from the café, leaving his coffee behind and a wet spot on the chair.

Po Po doubled over and laughed. "This will be the last time he tries to put the squeeze on my girl." Raina joined her grandma's laughter until tears rolled down her face. "Did you see the stains on his white jacket?"

After a few minutes, they cleaned up the leather reading chair. The owner must have put some kind of stain guard on it because it wiped clean. Raina grabbed her grandma's beach-size purse, and they left the café with linked arms.

"How much of our conversation did you hear?" Raina asked.

"Most of it. The two of you were so focused on each other, you didn't see me sit down," Po Po said with a hint of pride in her voice. "Pay attention to your surroundings, Rainy. The murderer could sneak up on you, especially with everyone walking around in costumes. The killer could be watching us now."

Raina glanced around uneasily. She didn't like this idea at all. "I haven't had lunch yet. Let's go get some food."

"Sounds good. Maggie and Frank went off to book their big day at the chapel. They don't have time for the likes of us," Po Po said.

Raina gave her grandma a sideways glance. "Do I detect jealousy in your voice? Don't tell me you're in love with Frank?"

"Nooo! Ewww. He's just a friend."

"Sounds like someone is protesting too much."

"I'm not jealous, but Maggie is my best friend. Now she's his best friend."

"I doubt he'll replace fifty years of friendship."

"You don't understand, Rainy. Maggie and I are like Thelma and Louise. Rice and egg rolls. It's just not right to separate us."

If they were having this conversation under different circumstances, Raina might let her grandma go on for a bit. However, this was not normal. They were dealing with a murder investigation, and she didn't have time to play armchair psychiatrist to her grandma's quirky logic. What her grandma needed was tough love.

"You're being really selfish here," Raina whispered.

Po Po frowned. "No—"

"You're always jetting off between San Francisco, Morrow Cliff Village to visit Lucy, and back home. You're always visiting family, but think about poor Maggie. She only has Matthew."

"She's always welcome to come along."

"But they're still not her family."

"Close enough. She's been part of the family for fifty years. She knows all my relatives."

Raina shook her head. "It's still not the same. And Frank has only one granddaughter. They could keep each other company during those times when she wants to stay put. You should be happy they have each other."

Po Po blushed. By this time, they were in line for the buffet. Her grandma was silent, deep in thought.

Raina gave her grandma the space to process what she had said. Her grandma was usually the most generous woman she knew, but there were times when she could be selfish as well, especially when it meant things would change for her.

After they paid for the buffet and got inside the restaurant, Po Po broke their silence. "You're right, Rainy. I'm an old fool."

Raina's heart clenched at the droopy look on her grandma's face. She gave her a hug. "No, never a fool. Just someone blinded by love. And Maggie and Frank are both very lucky to have you as their best friend."

Po Po brightened. "Maybe I can be a bridesmaid. I better go check on them after lunch. Maggie can't see very well anymore, and I know her taste better than anyone. She'll need my help to pick out a dress."

Raina broke into a wide grin. "I thought you were my Watson. What am I supposed to do without my wing woman?" She set their receipt on the table to claim their booth.

"You seem to be doing fine without me. Just don't let that handsome detective turn your head. He's up to no good. You're lucky I got here when I did."

"And how would you know this?"

"I think he was on the news a couple of years ago for something. I'm sure if we search his name on the Internet, we'll find something nefarious."

They split up and made their way to the various stations to grab food. When Raina slid into the booth, Po Po was digging into a huge plate of French fries drowning in nacho cheese sauce. How was it possible that her grandma still had the digestion and appetite of a teenager?

Raina picked at her salad, moving the lettuce leaves around. After one or two bites, she dug into the two beef tacos on the other plate. She groaned at the savory bite. Now this was more like it.

"Hey, I have news from the Science Ninjas," Po Po said. "They were able to crack the password protection on the USB stick."

"Wow, that was fast. We were only talking about it this morning. How did you even get the USB to them this quickly?"

"Courier service. Hand delivered an hour ago."

Raina's eyes widened. And these kids cracked the password lock already? Yikes! She was both awed and horrified at what could happen if these kids worked for the bad guys. "How did you even have time to arrange all this? I thought you were in the guitar seminar this morning."

"I only stayed for the first ten minutes. It was so boring. They were talking about fingering techniques. If I could move my hands like that, playing a guitar would be the last thing on my mind."

Raina blinked. She wasn't sure if her grandma meant to imply something naughty, but it was best if she ignored the comment. "So what did the Science Ninjas find on the USB stick?"

"NASA's research and plans for a super drone that could spray pesticides on crops to replace the duster planes."

"I thought that technology was already widely available."

"The ones on the market are for short distance and at low elevations. The super drone has a range of over three hundred miles and the ability to avoid detection."

Raina's heart sank. Her grandma just confirmed that Matthew was up to his armpits in the NASA information breach. Was he trying to recover the USB or buying it for someone else? "If the technology falls into the wrong hands, this could cause extensive damage to a large area."

"Not if they are spraying happy gas. Some people at the senior center could use some of that."

Raina ignored the comment. "I wonder if this is Gloria's research. She accused Claire of stealing it."

"I don't understand why it ended up in your room."

"My guess is that Claire was supposed to deliver the USB stick to Matthew in the laundry room, but when Gloria showed up, Claire got spooked. So she decided it would be safer to drop it off in Matthew's room."

"Why didn't she just call Matthew to move the rendezvous up?"

"Who knows? Maybe she couldn't get in touch with him."

"Does this mean she didn't expect you to be in the room?"

"She certainly seemed surprised when I called out to her, but she moved like a ninja. And how could you miss a big lump on the bed? She probably knew I was in the room but thought she could do her business without waking me."

"How did she know what room you're in? Or that you're Matthew's fiancée?"

Raina blushed. "Well, I was stupid enough to give her my name and room number the day before. I was trying to get us tickets for the convention. My name must have caught her attention because she made a comment about it. And I told her my fiancé's name was Matthew."

Po Po raised an eyebrow. "And you get on my case about spilling the beans?"

Now heat engulfed Raina from the neck up. "Hey, I'm following the example of my elders."

"I hope you don't mean me because I'm not that old. Only sixty. Not old enough to be an elder yet."

Raina gave her grandma a sideways glance. Her mother was fifty, so it was biologically impossible for her grandma to have her youngest child at ten years old. She dismissed thoughts of her grandma's age.

She shifted her thoughts to Matthew. Why was he getting stolen technology from Claire? Was he a middleman, picking it up for someone else? And was this buyer one of the bad guys?

Po Po studied Raina's face. "Are you okay? What are you thinking?"

Raina told her grandma her thoughts.

"Russian spies? Terrorist groups? Any one of them would want the technology," Po Po said.

Raina shook her head. "No way. Matthew is one of the good guys. He would never help them. Maybe he was trying to get the stolen information back to NASA. He did say he was working on a security job."

"Should I tell the kids to overnight the USB stick back to us? This could be a matter of national security, and I don't want the kids to be involved any longer than necessary."

Raina shook her head. "We can't risk the USB getting lost in the mail. Can they drop it off with someone at the senior center?" She didn't want to get the senior citizens involved either, but she trusted the Posse Club members more than she did these high school kids.

The Posse Club was her grandma's brainchild. They were a group of active senior citizens with a warped sense of humor who liberally used stink bombs to get back at their nemeses. And they also monitored everything that happened in town.

"I'll tell the kids to drop it off with the Lovebirds, and they can lock it in my safe," Po Po said. The Lovebirds was the code name for a couple who had been married for a gazillion years.

"But don't tell them what's on the USB stick. If the authorities ask, the Lovebirds could still say they were only doing a favor for their friend," Raina said.

Po Po pulled out her cell phone, and her fingers flew across the screen, sending out messages to her minions. When she was done, she asked, "What's next, Sherlock?"

"Now we have to find Gloria, our NASA girl," Raina said.

Gloria had plenty of motive for killing Claire. When the security breach became common knowledge, Gloria could kiss her career goodbye. She might have murdered Claire for revenge.

9

AN UNLIKELY PAIR

They headed toward the convention area. Raina was so focused on tracking down Gloria Tanaka that she didn't even realize her grandma was no longer by her side. One minute Po Po was there, and the next she was gone. Raina spun around, her gaze scanning the casino floor.

There! Her grandma was skulking behind a bank of slot machines and peering around the corner with her birdwatching binoculars. Did Po Po think she could be inconspicuous in her cone bra and sundress?

Raina marched up to her grandma and tapped on her shoulder. "What are you doing?"

"Shhh!" Po Po pointed a finger at the blackjack table in front of them.

Raina rolled her eyes. As if anyone could hear them over the music, clanging slot machines, and the cheering crowds. Her gaze followed her grandma's finger. "Am I supposed to recognize somebody at the blackjack table?"

Po Po shoved the birdwatching binoculars into Raina's hands. "At the Lone Star Saloon. In the corner."

Raina peered with the binoculars at the booth in the corner of the bar area. She gasped. Willie and Brian were huddled close together in the shadows. There might be enough distance to slide a sheet of paper between them.

Willie had changed out of her power suit and into a dress that made her grandma's sundress modest in comparison. She had also lost her tawny blonde coloring and wore a long black wig with straight bangs like a stereotypical Asian woman. Since Brian was such a slight man, she looked like an Amazon next to him. He had dispensed with his toupee, and his shiny bald head gleamed in the faint light, contrasting with his dark sideburns. He was flushed like he was excited. Maybe it was from the attention of an attractive woman.

Raina assumed he knew the woman was Willie, but she didn't know if he had glanced up from her chest long enough to pay any attention to her face. "I can't believe those two are a couple. I wonder how long it has been going on."

Someone tapped Raina on the shoulder. She lowered the binoculars and turned to see Hendricks frowning at her. "Yes?" she asked.

"What are you doing?" Hendricks asked. His tall

square body blocked Raina's view. His hooded eyes hid his thoughts. "Are you helping someone cheat?"

Raina glanced around. Her grandma had pulled a disappearing act, leaving Raina to explain the spying and binoculars. Some wing woman.

"No cheating here. I see someone at the Lone Star Saloon who looks suspiciously like Willie, except she's wearing a wig and a skimpy dress," Raina said. "I'm just taking a closer look." She wiggled her binoculars like this should be self-explanatory.

Hendricks didn't even blink. "What the boss does in her personal time is her business."

"So Willie does this often? Why is she necking with the convention organizer? It seems rather distasteful to do this so publicly after one of their own was just murdered."

"Like I said, that's her personal business. Now move on out of here before I bring you into the office and call the cops on your suspicious behavior," Hendricks said.

"Hey, we never got around to seeing the video feed outside the hallway of my suite. I want to know how Claire Boucher got into my suite the morning of her death."

Raina didn't believe there would be any video surveillance, but she wanted to ask anyway. If nothing else, the head of security could confirm her theory. And maybe if she made him squirm, he might be open to the suggestion they partner up for this investigation.

The head of security wasn't her first choice of a

partner, but she didn't trust Detective Stafford. And while Po Po might think the two of them were equal to any professional, they didn't have what it took to take down the real killer. And a big tank of a guy like Hendricks might come in handy with his muscles.

Hendricks didn't exactly blush, but he stiffened. "There is no video outside of your room. Some of the cameras are decoys."

Raina stared at him for a long moment. It was just as she suspected. "I assume you don't want this to become common knowledge around here."

"Are you threatening me?"

"Of course not. I just want to make sure we're on the same page."

He made a sound halfway between a snort and a grunt.

"How is that investigation on Claire Boucher's death coming along? I keep seeing Detective Stafford and his staff all over the hotel," Raina said, exaggerating the police presence. "I'm surprised Willie isn't more concerned."

"What's in this for you? Are you trying to cover up for your fiancé?"

"I have no stake in this, and that man is not my fiancé. But I am curious why Claire came into my room before her death. She didn't appear to take or leave anything behind."

He gave her an appraising look. "You look to be about my niece's age, so here's a piece of advice. Stay out of this. Enjoy your vacation and then go home."

"Unfortunately, I have a grandmother who loves to read murder mystery books. And since I didn't fall far from the apple tree, I am also curious."

"Well, it's your neck. Don't say I didn't warn you. I would hate to find you stuffed in a laundry bag."

Raina shivered at the horrid thought. "Don't you want this business to clear up as quickly as possible?"

Hendricks shrugged. "I don't particularly care."

"If Willie finds out about the security holes in your department, you might care then."

He scowled at her. "Are you threatening me?"

She suppressed the urge to roll her eyes. The man was starting to sound like a broken record. "No. I'm trying to save your bacon. Like you said, at the end of my vacation, I'm going home. But with you, you'll have to deal with the fallout from the police investigation. I'm not sure you want them to talk to Willie about the gaps in your security."

Hendricks appeared to consider her words. His brows furrowed into deep lines on his face. "What are you proposing?"

"I'm not sure. If you see anything suspicious, maybe we should talk about it. I'm good at connecting the dots, and I don't need any credit for capturing the murderer."

"Why me? Shouldn't you work with the police?"

"The police don't need a nosy civilian," Raina said. "Besides, if you get news coverage of the takedown, think about what it could do for your career. Maybe you could spin this somehow. Transform yourself into an elite security consultant for other hotel-casinos. Imagine that."

Hendricks frowned for a long moment as if considering her words. When he finally held out his hand, it was all Raina could do to keep from doing a fist pump at the victory.

"As long as I get to take down the bad guy," he said. They shook hands on the deal.

WHEN RAINA GOT AWAY from the casino floor and into the convention area, she texted her grandma.

WHERE ARE YOU?

Her grandma replied.

SORRY. I HAD A WARDROBE MALFUNCTION. A CONE FELL OFF. I'M WITH MAGGIE MAKING WEDDING ARRANGEMENTS.

Raina blinked at the message. Nope, she didn't misread the words. Sometimes she wondered if it was worth the trouble of having her grandma tag along in these investigations. Not that she was brave enough to say no to her grandma.

She put the phone away and headed toward the plastic table still in front of the main hall. There was no one there. She pulled out the program from her purse and looked at the events for today. It was a battle of the bands on stage. The exhibit hall was also open. And there was a film playing in one of the smaller conference rooms. That was a lot of ground for Raina to cover on her own.

Raina went into the main hall and walked along the edge until she was next to the stage, waiting for the amateur band to finish playing. She would have to take a page of her grandma's playbook.

A few minutes later and after the applause died down, the amateur band gathered their instruments to get off the stage. There were a few minutes of intermission while the next band set up.

Raina ran on stage and grabbed the microphone. "Has anyone seen Gloria Tanaka? Got a message for her from her boss."

She squinted against the bright spotlight and scanned the crowd in front of her. People were getting up and moving around. But one lady stood up and pointed toward the exit sign on Raina's right. Underneath the sign was an alcove large enough for performers to mingle while they waited their turn to go on stage. Raina thanked the woman.

By the time Raina made her way down the steps and toward the alcove, the music started again, and Raina made her way toward where Gloria Tanaka was last seen. She ducked into the alcove, surprised at the dim light and the break on her ears from the boisterous music. The band on stage had more enthusiasm than rhythm. When her eyes adjusted to the dim light inside the alcove, Raina realized she wasn't alone.

Gloria, with stars in her eyes, was listening to a man who was delivering a speech that could change her life. He leaned into her personal space, twirling a strand of her hair with one finger. His mouth was inches from hers and no doubt Gloria could breathe in each one of his breaths. She was ready for seduction.

Heat rose to Raina's face. She didn't want to watch what would happen next. In her mind, she could hear Po Po's voice singing "Super Freak." She took a step closer and cleared her throat. "Gloria, we need to talk before the police arrest you for Claire Boucher's murder."

The man stiffened. He glanced at Raina and then back at Gloria, the smile frozen on his face. "I should get back to Brian."

"I'll come with you," Gloria said, ignoring Raina. Though her voice sounded sweet and unconcerned, the hand holding her purse strap tightened into a white-knuckled grip.

"I know who stole the super drone research," Raina said.

Gloria's head swiveled toward Raina. Her eyes widened in surprise. "What did you say?"

"Meet me in the hallway," Raina said. She marched out of the alcove. The ball was now in Gloria's court, and Raina had no doubt the NASA woman would want to play.

Fifteen minutes later, Raina was still in the hallway

by herself. She glanced at the digital display on her cell phone again. Even if Gloria wanted a quickie with her friend, she would have been done by now.

As Raina trotted to the alcove again, she berated herself for her arrogance. She had assumed Gloria's curiosity would be as strong as hers for finding answers. After all, Gloria was a NASA researcher. Wasn't curiosity a requirement for the job? And this was her livelihood at stake. Wouldn't she want information about the person who stole her research?

Instead, Raina probably spooked the NASA researcher. Unsurprisingly, the alcove was empty. She would have to start her search for Gloria all over again.

10

———

WRONG MOVE

Raina collapsed onto her bed, stuffed to the gills. Dinner with the senior citizens had been fun while they regaled her with their adventures at the wedding chapel and shopping for wedding clothes. She didn't discuss the case with them because the details were a jumbled mess in her mind.

Before she could work up the energy to take a shower, someone knocked on her door.

"It's me, Rainy," Po Po called out. "Let me in."

Raina groaned. As much as she loved her grandma, she was hoping for some quiet time. She got up and opened the door. Standing in the hallway was her grandma with a little red suitcase.

"Where are you going?" Raina asked.

Po Po stepped around Raina and came into the room, dragging the suitcase behind her. "Since Matthew isn't here, I'm moving in with you."

Raina closed the door and locked it. "Why?"

"Why do you think? It's awkward to be in the same room with Maggie and Frank."

"But you've shared a room with them before."

"That was before they got engaged. I don't want to be around when they do the lovey-dovey thing."

Raina could see why her grandma no longer felt comfortable with the sleeping arrangements. She glanced at the king-size bed. There wasn't enough room on there to escape her grandma's kangaroo legs when she was in a deep sleep. She sighed. Tomorrow she would need an extra coffee to get through the day.

Po Po unzipped her suitcase and made herself at home, pulling out her toiletries bag and shaking out her pajamas. "So what happened after I left you with Hendricks?"

Raina told her grandma about her deal with Hendricks and the miscalculation with Gloria.

"So who's on the suspect list now?" Po Po asked.

"There's Brian Anderson. His name badge was found near the scene of the crime. He is not exactly a big guy, so he could have dressed up as the killer maid."

"But what is his motive?"

"The missing ten thousand dollars? Organizing the convention is his only link to Claire."

Po Po frowned. "If Claire had stolen the money from the convention, why would he kill her for it?"

Raina got back onto the bed and watched her grandma move about the room. "What if Claire didn't steal the money? What if Brian did? He was the original convention organizer. Claire only filled in because he got sick. What if she found out about the missing money and confronted him about it?"

"That's a good theory, but she was a thief herself. Why does it matter to her if Brian stole money?"

"Maybe she was blackmailing him? This could be an opportunity to squeeze blood out of a turnip."

"Who else is on your list? The NASA woman?"

Raina nodded. "Gloria Tanaka's livelihood is at stake. She believes Claire stole her super drone research. She came to this convention to confront Claire but probably didn't get anywhere. She could have killed Claire in a fit of anger."

"How did Gloria know Claire would be in the laundry room?"

Raina stared off into space for a moment. Someone had mentioned something. She swung her legs out of bed, grabbed her purse, and pulled out her little notebook. She flipped through the pages until she got to her conversation with the costume saleswoman. "Claire lost her cell phone before her death."

Po Po raised an eyebrow. "Oookay. What am I supposed to do with this information?"

"Maybe Gloria stole Claire's cell phone. Or one of the other suspects did."

Po Po's eyes widened. "And hacked into her emails or text messages. This could explain how the killer maid knew about the rendezvous location and got there before Matthew and Claire did."

"And now there is Willie," Raina said. "I didn't see

this coming. From my conversation with Hendricks, it sounded like she role-played fairly often in her free time. But why would she do it at work?"

Po Po shrugged. "Maybe she hates her job? Maybe she's pushing the boundaries to see how much it would take for them to fire her? Who knows?"

"And how serious is her relationship with Brian? Would she kill for him?"

Po Po shrugged. "That's above my pay grade, Sherlock. You're the brains of this operation." She pulled something out of her suitcase and tossed it on the bed. "I got you a stun gun."

Her grandma often supplied Raina with weapons of mass destruction. Some items were homemade by the Science Ninjas Club, and others were bought off the Internet.

"Is this legal?" Raina asked, eyeing the lipstick tube doubtfully.

"If a three hundred pound man is coming after you, would you care?" Po Po asked.

"No."

"There's enough voltage to curl his chest hair." Po Po cackled like it was the funniest joke ever.

"Do I need to charge it?"

"It's fully charged."

Raina put the stun gun on the bedside table. She never used one of these before, but she would add it to the drawer of gadgets in her dresser at home.

Po Po went into the bathroom to shower and get

ready for bed. While Raina had hoped for some solitude, she understood why her grandma came over.

However, having her grandma in the suite only reminded Raina of Matthew's absence even more acutely. By herself, she could pretend her fiancé would return any night now. With her grandma in the room, there was no pretense left.

Raina's cell phone rang, and she pulled it out of her purse. When she saw the caller ID, her heart leapt to her throat. She tapped on the screen to take the call with a shaking hand.

"Matthew?" she whispered.

"Hi, Rainy," Matthew said. He sounded exhausted like he hadn't had a decent night of sleep in a while.

"Are you done with your freelance job? When can I see you again?" The words tumbled out of her mouth, making her sound needier than she wanted to appear.

"Um, there is no freelance job."

Raina blinked, trying to process what he'd just said. "Where are you?"

"Home," Matthew said.

"Seriously, where are you?"

There was a long pause.

Raina took a deep breath, but it didn't calm her down. Maybe he was being obtuse because the line wasn't secured. If he really were in Gold Springs, she wasn't sure what she would do to him the next time she saw him. Heat rose to her cheeks along with her rising anger. "Well?"

"The Chief called, and I had to go. I was hoping

you wouldn't notice. I was planning to come back on the weekend to pick you up." Matthew was a homicide detective in their hometown.

"You think I wouldn't notice my fiancé ditched me in a hotel room? With the grandmas?" Raina asked, not bothering to hide the irritation in her voice.

"Sorry." He sounded sincere.

Raina couldn't believe this. Did the man think an apology would be enough for what he did? For his abandonment?

"Go have a good time. Charge whatever you need to the room. I've got to go. I have to respond to an emergency. Love you, Rainy," Matthew said. His voice sounded far away like he was already back on his police work.

Raina stared at the phone. How could he do this to her? She thought they were getting married in Las Vegas. She even packed a lovely dress for the cere-mony. "Are you planning to come back?"

There was a long pause again.

"Can you book a flight home?" he finally asked tentatively.

She could imagine him ducking from an invisible blow because that was what she felt like doing to him at this moment. "If you don't come back here, the engagement is off."

Raina hung up without waiting for an answer. He was such a selfish jerk. Not only did he leave her behind, but he also left his grandma behind. His half-blind grandma.

She blinked at the burning tears in her eyes. She got herself involved in a murder investigation because she wanted to help him—the bearded man from the video feed. When all along, he had been home working. She understood dedication to the job, but this was going too far. She couldn't very well elope without a groom.

Po Po stepped out of the bathroom. "Who were you talking to?"

"Oh, I've been such a fool," Raina said. The tears spilled down her cheeks. She normally wasn't one of those weepy women, but she was so frustrated at this impasse in their relationship again.

Po Po handed Raina a tissue and listened. Everything came tumbling out: her fear of Matthew's involvement, the bearded man coming outside of the laundry room, and her conversation with Matthew.

"I don't understand how he can do this to me," Raina said. "If he was involved with the murder investigation, I could forgive him for not being here. I thought he was trying to protect us by keeping away from us, but for him to just go home and resume his life? I don't know what to think."

"What else did he say?" Po Po asked.

"He wants me to fly home with the two of you and the dog." The more Raina thought about the situation, the angrier she got. She wiped the tears off her face.

"Let's think this through," Po Po said, sounding way too calm. Normally, her grandma would be the one who was quicker to anger and plot revenge.

Raina crossed her arms and snapped her mouth shut. Fine. If her grandma didn't want to hear her whine, she could berate Matthew in her mind. But it didn't make sense for Matthew to leave Las Vegas without them. If he had to drive back to Gold Springs for work, why didn't they all check out and go home together?

And Raina and the grandmas were the only family he had. He would move heaven and earth to see them safe and out of harm's way. Leaving them in Sin City with no transportation and no idea of when he would return wasn't the kind of thing he would normally do.

Wait a minute. Did he tell her a white lie, hoping she would get on a plane to go home? Now, this would be more like him.

"What is it, Rainy?" Po Po asked. "You look like you had a brain fart?"

Raina ignored her grandma's comment. "I think he is trying to get us out of Las Vegas."

"Um, are you sure?" Po Po asked doubtfully.

"First, his grandma is half blind. There is no way he would abandon her anywhere. Think about it. When you visit the Bay Area, you and Maggie have to leave town first and then call to let him know you are gone. If he knows about your trips beforehand, he tries to talk you out of it or wants to tag along."

"He hovers like a mother hen."

"Second, he tells me he's at home. So naturally, I would run home to yell at him."

Po Po laughed. "Yes, I can see reverse psychology here."

"I think he is still here at the hotel. He sounds exhausted like he's been catching cat naps here and there."

"Well, if he is still at the hotel, it's not like he could book another room using his identity if he's working incognito."

Raina's worry returned like the blast of a bomb. Her poor fiancé. Normally, when he worked a case, he had a team helping him out. With this freelance gig, he had to do it alone, worry about his family, and probably sleep like a homeless person around the casino-hotel.

"And don't forget about the bearded man in the video feed. He moves like Matthew," Raina said.

"Oookay, but I still don't understand what all this means."

"I think something went deadly wrong with his freelance gig. And now he's trying to fix it and hoping we'll get out of here before things get out of hand."

"You mean Claire Boucher's death?" Po Po asked.

Raina nodded.

Po Po took a moment to process what Raina said. "Do you think we should check out in the morning? I don't know if we can get a flight home this quickly."

"I don't know. He's working this case alone. Yes, we could potentially get in the way, but we can also help him."

"He's not going to want your help."

Raina's jaw tightened. "Until he surfaces, he won't have much of a choice. He said I should have a good time, so that's what I plan to do."

"Are you going shopping tomorrow?"

"No, shopping is no fun."

"Then what's fun?"

"Squeezing the suspects for answers."

11

POOF

The next morning, Raina woke to another hot desert day. She got to sleep in because she didn't have to wake at the crack of dawn to walk Poe, Maggie's service dog, and wait for him to do his business. Now the task fell on Frank. It was a nice change.

As she went through her morning routine, she took special care to look her best, putting on both mascara and lipstick. Matthew was somewhere in the hotel and probably in disguise like most of the people at the convention. He didn't want to break off their elopement after all. He was keeping his distance to protect her. She hummed under her breath. This she could handle.

Her grandma knocked on the bathroom door. "Did we get the laundry back yet? I want to get back into my red jumpsuit."

Raina opened the door. "The tag said we'd get

them back before nine if we drop them off before eight last night."

"It's nine twenty already. I don't think we'll get our costumes back before lunch."

"We'll have to go down to the laundry room and have a look-see. The costumes are as good an excuse as any."

Po Po grinned. "I like how you think."

They got dressed and headed downstairs.

While they waited for the elevator, Po Po asked, "So what's the plan for today?"

"The same plan we have every day. Conquer the world."

"You know what I mean. Are you going to look for Matthew?"

Raina shook her head. "If he wants to be found, he would make it easy for us to find him. In the meantime, he'll see that we're out and about, which means we're not leaving. So at some point, he'll have to seek us out."

They got into the elevator and got out at the casino floor. They casually made their way to the service hall. As they walked through the double swinging doors, Raina saw Brian Anderson coming out of the laundry room and heading straight towards them to go back to the casino floor. It was her lucky day. She didn't have to track him down.

"Are you here to pick up your costume? I didn't get mine this morning either," Raina said.

Brian glanced over, startled. Then his shoulders

relaxed, but he frowned at her. "You look familiar. Do I know you?"

Raina shook her head. "We haven't been introduced, but I know you because you are the convention organizer, and I've been coming to the convention for years." She held out her hand. "I'm Raina Sun. And this is my grandma, Bonnie Wong. It's nice to meet you. Thank you for putting on such a fantastic show all these years."

Brian shook her hand but continued to frown. "I've seen you somewhere before."

Raina flushed. Should she confess to eavesdropping on his conversation with Detective Stafford? Before she could make up her mind on what to say next, her grandma cut in.

"Say, what happened to the ten thousand dollars? Did Claire Boucher take it? And if she did, do you think it's still somewhere in the hotel-casino?" Her grandma's eyes gleamed. "Can you imagine if this convention turned into a scavenger hunt for the money?"

Brian's eyes widened, and he inched back from them.

"Po Po, why don't you check on the costumes?" Raina said, giving her grandma a pointed stare. If her grandma kept up with her questions, Brian would hightail it out of here.

Po Po marched off, clearly put out. If she were a cat, her tail would be high in the air like a lightning rod.

"Please excuse my grandma. She's a little senile,"

Raina said, using her grandma's favorite excuse for her unconventional behavior. "Are the police planning to question the attendees about Claire Boucher's death?" She wrung her hands, pretending to be anxious.

"Unfortunately there's nothing I can do to stop them from questioning the attendees. Just answer their questions honestly and try your best to forget about the incident."

Raina knew he was trying to reassure her as any good leader might after a disaster, but his words sounded so cold. Didn't Brian work together with Claire before? Or belong to the same social circles with their common interest in rock-and-roll?

She pretended to glance at his name badge for the first time. "Hey, what happened to your name badge?" She pointed at her badge. "I have to write my name in because I registered late. But where's your printed badge?"

"I must have misplaced it. I've been busy playing catch-up since I got here."

Raina pointed at the side exit next to the laundry room behind them. "Your name badge is outside."

Brian turned around. "Outside?"

Raina nodded. "Underneath the hedge. It was found there on the day that Claire Boucher got strangled. The police seem to think that's the path the killer took to leave the scene of the crime."

Brian licked his lower lip. "I don't know how it got there."

Raina studied him for a long moment. "I think you

were standing out there on the day she died. I don't know what you were doing or if you were waiting for her, but you were out there."

Brian took a step back from her. "I don't have to answer any questions. You have no right to question my whereabouts."

"I know. I'm just a nosy murder mystery reader. But if I can figure this out on my own, what makes you think the police haven't caught on to the same thing?" She pointed at the cameras above them in the smoky glass half domes. She lowered her voice to a whisper. "And Big Brother is watching."

Brian swiveled on his heels and trotted down the service hall toward the casino floor.

Raina didn't know how to interpret his reaction. If he was the killer maid, he could have lost the badge before he hid in the laundry room. She studied his retreating back. He was slender, about one hundred fifty pounds or so and short enough to pass for a woman with the right disguise. A bra stuffed with tissue like what her grandma did with the cone bra wouldn't look amiss from far away.

And even if he had nothing to do with Claire's death, he knew something...enough to make him nervous. For one thing, if he had thought it through, his first question should be how Raina found out about his name badge. For all he knew, she could have been the killer.

～

RAINA AND PO PO went upstairs and changed into their costumes. Then they headed to the diner for breakfast with Maggie and Frank. Over eggs, ham, and pancakes, they decided to split up to look for Gloria Tanaka. They were to call Raina if they found her. Neither Raina nor Po Po mentioned Matthew's phone call the night before.

"How do we know what Gloria looks like?" Frank asked.

Po Po pulled out her cell phone and tapped on the screen. Several cell phones chirped around the table. "I sent you her pictures."

Raina checked her phone. Her eyes widened. "So you have been wearing a digital camera." She studied her grandma. "Which one is the camera? The flower pin or the necklace?"

Po Po straightened, and her lips curled into a Mona Lisa smile. "If I tell you, I'll have to get rid of you. Or you'll need to self-destruct in three seconds."

Raina glanced at the photo again, studying the angle. Since the photos appeared to be snapped from below everyone's chin and off-center, the camera had to be hidden in... "It's your flower pin?"

"You guessed it. Now are you going to self-destruct?" Po Po said with laughter in her voice.

Raina held up a fist and spread her fingers. "Poof!"

Frank snorted at the interplay.

"Now for the more important topic. What are we going to do for the impersonation show?" Po Po asked. "Winners get their names splashed in the newspaper and the internet. Plus, there's a thousand-dollar cash prize and free tickets for next year's convention."

Both Frank and Maggie leaned forward as Po Po spoke, following her every word.

Raina dropped the napkin over her plate and pushed back her chair. "Well, I'm off to see Willie. She's probably in her office by now."

"Wait! Don't you want to be part of the show?" Maggie asked.

"I'll pass," Raina said, getting up. "I'll check in with you in an hour. If you don't hear from me, send in the cavalry."

As Raina made her way through the casino floor to the elevator, she rehearsed what she wanted to say to the general manager. With no authority to question the suspects, how was she to get Willie to talk?

In previous investigations, she had always relied on her relationships with the suspects or victim to get people to talk. In this case, everyone involved was a stranger, even the victim. If not for Matthew, she would have gladly left the case to Detective Stafford.

By the time Raina knocked on Willie's office door, she still had no idea how to handle the situation. She would have to trust her intuition on what to say.

Willie was tapping on the keyboard in front of her desk. She raised an eyebrow at Raina's appearance. "Can I help you with something?" Her gravelly tone implied she was too busy for this conversation.

Raina slid into the chair in front of the desk.

"I have a meeting in a few minutes," Willie said.

The general manager was in a white power suit with a low-cut red top underneath it. Her tawny blonde hair was coiled into a chignon. Raina couldn't see her shoes, but she had a feeling they were at least four-inch stiletto heels. Willie liked to tower over everyone.

Raina ignored the comment. Most people would back away in embarrassment for interrupting, but Raina didn't work for Willie. She didn't care how much of the general manager's time she was taking up with her questions.

"Brian Anderson is in trouble," Raina said, going for the shock factor. Maybe the news would rattle the general manager into spilling some useful information. "His name badge was found under a hedge outside in the delivery dock area after someone strangled Claire Boucher."

Willie raised an eyebrow. "Why would I care about this person's badge? Is he on the payroll? And why did the police give you this information?"

"Weren't you exchanging saliva with Brian at the bar last night? I thought you might want to warn him before the police connect the murder to him."

"I'm not sure why you think I would care," Willie said, ignoring Raina's comment about her extracurricular activities. Talk about nerves of steel. "If you have anything to say about the investigation, go to the police or my head of security." She stood and gestured at the doorway.

Raina settled into the chair. "You mean Hendricks?

He can't even find his way out of a trash bag. I'm not saying he's incompetent, but he's used to reporting on suspicious activity to the police and escorting people outside the property. This is way above his pay grade."

Willie narrowed her eyes at Raina. "So why are you involved in this investigation?"

Raina suppressed the urge to shiver. If Willie had anything to do with Claire Boucher's death, it might not be a good idea to antagonize her too much. "I'm just a nosy nobody who loves a murder mystery."

"Well, Miss Nosy, I would be careful where you stick your nose. This is not a story where nothing bad can happen to you. The big bad wolf has sharp teeth here in Las Vegas."

Raina accepted the warning with a nod. "Got it. I'll make sure to tell the police about your involvement with Brian Anderson and your tendency to play dress up. I don't know if Hendricks told you, but the killer dressed up as one of your maids. That's how she could hide out in the laundry room without anyone raising a peep."

Willie stiffened at the implied threat. "Half the people here are in costume."

"But only a few know the maid schedule or have access to their uniforms."

"A black T-shirt with our hotel logo isn't exactly hard to get your hands on. Besides, I was in a meeting at the time of Claire's death."

"But what about Brian Anderson? Does he have an alibi?"

"I don't like how you keep linking our names together. Brian Anderson has been coming to our hotel-casino for the last ten years for his convention. We have an excellent working relationship. But that's it."

Raina raised an eyebrow. Did she detect a hint of defensiveness in the general manager's voice? "When I mentioned the name badge, you said you don't know Brian Anderson. But now you have a good working relationship with him. So which one is it?"

"Sorry, I didn't make the connection." Willie pretended to laugh. "I didn't have enough coffee this morning. As for Brian, I don't know if he has an alibi or not. But why do you think he has anything to do with Claire's death?"

"His name badge was found outside in the loading dock. And that's where the maid came in." Raina didn't know if this was true or not, but it sounded plausible. For all she knew, he could have been out there waiting for things to unload for the convention and dropped his name badge.

"Well, I hope it's not him. He seems like a good guy." Willie typed on her keyboard, clearly dismissing Raina.

"Good to know. I wouldn't want him arrested either. He does seem like a nice guy." Raina pushed herself up from the chair. "Thank you for your time."

While Willie didn't appear rattled from what Raina had revealed in the office, it might be a good idea to keep an eye on the general manager to see what she did next with the information.

Raina found a bench in a pay phone niche next to the elevator. A panel on the wall covered up what used to be wiring for the ancient device. She texted the Posse Club about her conversation with Willie. But before she could get into the details, movement from the corner of her eye caught Raina's attention. She leaned out for a look-see.

A woman with long straight black hair stepped out of Willie's office. She was wearing a strappy red tank top and Daisy Dukes jean shorts. Instead of the stilettos heels, she was in flat sneakers. It looked like Willie was in her disguise again. How could she think that people wouldn't recognize her?

Willie glanced up and down the hall. Raina ducked back into the niche and held her breath. Footsteps came towards her and the elevator area. The elevator dinged upon its arrival. Raina leaned out from the niche to see a Little Richie impersonator stepping out from the elevator and Willie stepping in. Raina ducked back into the niche and texted the Posse Club.

WILLIE IS IN HER DISGUISE AGAIN. SHE'S GOING DOWN THE ELEVATOR.

Her cell phone dinged with an incoming message.

WE ARE ON IT, SHERLOCK.

When the elevator closed, Raina came out to find the elevator area emptied. She glanced at the numbers on top of the elevator, but instead of going to the first floor, it stopped on the second floor.

Raina grabbed her phone and texted the Posse Club again.

WILLIE IS ON THE SECOND FLOOR. WHAT'S ON THE SECOND FLOOR?

Her phone vibrated.

THE INFINITY POOL.

Raina pushed the call button for the elevator. It looked like she might catch Willie having a little rendezvous with Brian after her vehement denial. She snorted at the thought of their professional relationship. The two of them were like peanut butter and jelly, so the two of them might have planned the murder together.

12

OPERATION PHOTO SHOOT

Willie strolled up to the wicker patio set in front of the rooftop pool. Detective Stafford sat on the wicker chair wearing a white polo shirt and jeans. Two mugs of coffee sat on the glass-top table. He rose from the chair and greeted Willie with a long kiss. Their meeting was like a scene from a movie set, romantic and sappy, with the light streaming in from behind them and the potted plants and flowers around them. Except this was Las Vegas, and everything from the landscaping to Willie's hair was a mirage.

If Raina needed any more proof that Detective Stafford wasn't an upstanding citizen, this would be it. Wasn't it a conflict of interest to investigate his girlfriend's hotel-casino? And just how many men was Willie seeing at the same time? And why would she want to conduct this personal business at work?

From the other side of the pool, Raina crouched

under a potted palm tree and pulled out the wig that came with the jumpsuit costume. She put the wig and a pair of sunglasses on, hoping this attempt at a disguise would be sufficient to hide her identity in a passing glance.

A commotion to Raina's right drew her attention, and she glanced over. Her jaw dropped. What in the world?

Frank and Maggie held hands and made their way to the edge of the infinity pool close to Willie and Detective Stafford. Frank was in a white tuxedo, and Maggie wore a full-length beige dress. Po Po wore a blonde wig and had a massive camera hung around her scrawny neck. A bored teenager followed them around, holding a reflector at the happy couple.

Several thoughts raced through Raina's mind. How in the world were the three of them able to get into their outfits so quickly? And did Frank and Maggie get married without Matthew or Raina? And where did the teenager come from?

After the initial glance, Willie and Detective Stafford ignored the bridal party and resumed their conversation. He held her hand on the table the entire time. What Raina wouldn't give to listen in on what they said. Luckily, her grandma was probably close enough to catch snatches of the conversation. She hoped the important stuff wouldn't get lost in translation when her grandma retold the conversation.

Po Po gestured for Maggie and Frank to get closer to the glass fencing behind the table. The teenager stood to the side, holding the reflector up with one hand and scrolling on his phone with the other. As Po Po looked through the viewfinder, she backed up until she was a foot from Willie and Detective Stafford.

Raina grinned. Her grandma was good. Perfect placement to listen in on everything. There wasn't much for her to do here. Maybe she should go back to the exhibit hall or the conference rooms to look for Gloria Tanaka. She was the only suspect that Raina hadn't spoken to yet.

Before Raina could slink away, Po Po backed up another foot until her rear tapped the wicker chair. Willie glanced behind her with a frown, removing her hand away from Detective Stafford. Po Po jerked and sidestepped. Her foot—the one with the bad ankle— stumbled on the edge of the infinity pool. She grabbed onto the back of the wicker chair. Willie shifted, twisting around with outstretched hands as if to hold back an attack. Po Po fell onto the wicker chair, knocking both Willie and the chair into the pool.

Willie screamed and hit the water with a splat. Ouch.

Po Po stopped her forward momentum by grabbing onto the table. Her hands splayed across the table and knocked the coffee mugs onto Detective Stafford's lap. He jerked back and twisted his body away from the hot liquid. His chair wobbled and tipped into the pool, spilling the detective into the water.

There was half a heartbeat of stunned silence. Po Po's eyes were the size of saucers. Willie bobbed up from the water, still screaming. Detective Stafford swam toward the general manager. By the time the two downed rats got out of the pool, the Posse Club was nowhere in sight.

Raina silently slinked away with suppressed laughter. So much for trying to find out what the two of them were chatting about in secret. She sighed. It looked like she was on her own. The Posse Club was no help after all.

RAINA MADE another trek to the exhibit hall, hoping to run into a suspect. She was expending a lot of energy going back and forth, and except for Willie, none of the suspects stayed in one spot for long. Without even being conscious of it, Raina had put all of the suspects on notice with her questions. It was much easier for them to track her down than the other way around. This was also more dangerous.

They were in the shadows while she was highly visible. And she was doing this on the assumption that Matthew was keeping tabs on her and would keep her safe. In hindsight, this was foolish. Her safety was her responsibility, and in unfamiliar surroundings, she should probably take precautions like carrying the lipstick stun gun with her.

Raina stopped by the costume booth. The saleswoman was friendly enough and a source of information. Maybe now that Claire Boucher's death was public knowledge, she might be more forthcoming with gossip.

The saleswoman was behind the booth showing a costume to a customer. The potential customer fingered the material and declared it was polyester and too cheaply made for the price. She left the booth in a huff when Joanne refused to sell the costume cheaper.

Raina waved at the saleswoman. "You doing okay?" She twirled. "I love my costume."

The saleswoman gave Raina a weary smile. "Looks good on you. Where's your grandma? Is she ready to buy another one yet?"

Raina held out her hand. "The name is Raina Sun."

The saleswoman shook hands. "Joanne Littleleaf."

Raina frowned. The saleswoman must have been a redhead in her youth because the freckles that once covered most of her face had blended in with the age spots. Her white hair was braided and wrapped around the crown of her head. The emerald green eyes held a depth of compassion like she had suffered through life rather than enjoyed it. But no matter how Raina looked at Joanne, she didn't look like a Native American.

"Littleleaf is my married name, in case you're wondering," Joanne said.

"Have you heard about what happened to Claire? The poor woman," Raina said.

"First, the convention is short on funds. And now this." Joanne sighed. "This is bad luck. My husband wants us to pack up and leave, but I didn't want to.

We paid too much as it is for this booth. And we usually go into the black from selling our merchandise here. If we leave now, we'll be hard-pressed to make a profit this year. And we need to make a profit this year."

"I'm sorry. My family owns small businesses, and I know what you mean about needing to make a profit. I thought you were doing this as a fun gig in your retirement."

Joanne laughed. It sounded harsh and bitter. "We have been doing this for the last twenty years. Being on the road and trying to raise a family is hard. We go from show to show. Now that the kids are grown, we're still doing this because we can't afford to retire."

Raina winced inwardly. The increased fee must have added to the Littleleafs worry like a ton of concrete. "Where's your husband now?"

"I'm not sure. He went to find Brian Anderson to see if we could get a partial refund on our fee. There's a lot less foot traffic than in previous years. It's obvious that Claire Boucher didn't do a good job advertising the show."

Raina pretended to glance around uneasily. "I'm spooked by the thought of a murderer walking among us. Who do you think killed Claire? She didn't seem like the type of woman to have a lot of enemies."

Joanne thought for a moment. "There's the Japanese woman who works with Claire at NASA. She is bad-mouthing Claire to everyone. And there's Brian Anderson. The convention lost ten thousand dollars.

The loss will go into next year's budget as well. It's a problem that will follow him around until it's paid off."

Raina frowned. "Is organizing the convention Brian Anderson's full-time job?"

"I don't know how it works. He organizes one here on the West Coast and one on the East Coast. I assume he does other events."

"Is the convention a for-profit event?"

Joanne chewed her lower lip, thinking about Raina's comment. "Actually, I think it's nonprofit. The fees are supposed to help fund a rock and roll memorabilia museum. There's a board for the museum, so I think it's a nonprofit."

"And Brian has been doing this for years?"

"At least for the last fifteen years. That's how long I've been coming here. Like I said, I bet he's mighty upset over the missing money. It wouldn't surprise me if he killed Claire for ruining the convention."

"Oh, I saw something interesting at the Lone Star Saloon last night," Raina said, lowering her voice to a whisper. "Do you know Willie Machado? The general manager of this hotel-casino?" At Joanne's nod, Raina continued, "She was in costume. A skimpy little dress with a long black wig." She paused. "She was sitting on Brian's lap, and they were pawing at each other."

Joanne's eyes widened. "From the way Willie talks to Brian, I thought she would rather poke him in the eye."

"Oh, really?"

"Willie threatened to stop reserving space for the

convention last year because of all the drinking and partying. It's a rock and roll convention. The partying kind of comes with the territory."

"Maybe this year she's trying it out for herself. Has the convention always been at this hotel?"

Joanne nodded. "Yes, but Willie has only been the manager for the last two years. I wonder if Brian seduced her so the convention could stay next year."

"Do you think Willie has anything to do with Claire's death?"

"What motive would she have for killing Claire?"

"I don't know. But isn't it strange she's suddenly friendly with Brian?" Raina asked.

"Not really. Brian can be quite a charming man. He would have to be to get all these vendors lining up to donate items for the gift baskets and money for his museum."

"Gift baskets?"

Joanne pointed to the stage at the front of the room. "You see all those gift baskets up there? They're all donations. Did you drop in your raffle ticket for the ones you want?"

"Where do I get the raffle tickets?"

"Everyone gets five raffle tickets as part of the fee, but you can purchase more on the stage. Brian is usually there with the baskets to keep an eye on things and sell more tickets."

Raina thanked Joanne for the chat and left when a customer came to ask about a velvet cape. She made her way to the stage, but it was closed for the day. A sign said it would be open tomorrow from eight to noon. She made a mental note to come back in the morning. At least now she knew where to find one of the suspects. If only she could smoke Gloria out for questioning.

13

ANOTHER EVENING SURPRISE

Raina jerked upright in bed. She glanced around the dark room. What had woken her? Her eyes flew to the doorway. A thin crack of light from the hallway spilled into the dark room. Someone had opened the door to her room and found it secured by the swing bar lock. After what happened with Claire Boucher, Raina wasn't taking any chances with someone creeping into her room. The person started to close the door.

She jumped out of bed, grabbed the lipstick stun gun and powered it on. It crackled to life, but her grandma's snoring must have hidden the sound from the intruder. She tiptoed up to the door, keeping away from the line of sight.

The door closed and opened again to a small sliver. A plastic card slid in and prodded at the swing bar lock. Was this the "Do Not Disturb" sign hanging outside on the doorknob? The flexible card bent around the swing bar and nudged it open. This person knew what he or she was doing.

Po Po continued to snore with no care in the world, but Raina's heartbeat sounded loud in her ears. She could scream and alert the person on the other side of the door. He or she would probably beat a hasty retreat at finding someone awake in the room.

Raina kept silent. She had no idea who would want to come into her room in the middle of the night, and she didn't care. She would figure it out once the intruder was no longer a threat.

The door widened and swung open. When Raina saw a hand holding a penlight, she lunged forward and touched the exposed skin. She winced as the hand tightened on the penlight. The hand tried to jerk back, but Raina pushed against the door with her body, trapping the hand in place and keeping it connected to the stun gun. She only had to hold on for two or three seconds.

When the hand went slack, she opened the door and brought up the heel of her palm, connecting it with the intruder's face just like her fiancé had taught her. His head flew back, hitting the doorframe. *Bam!*

With the hallway light behind him, his face was hidden by the shadow. Raina kicked him in the groin for good measure.

The man doubled over and fell to one knee. His breaths came out in loud heaving puffs. When he could finally speak, he gasped, "It's me, Rainy. Stop."

Raina hesitated, her fist suspended in midair. She

stepped back, bouncing on the balls of her feet, ready to zap him again when his words registered. "Matthew?"

"I don't think we can have children after this," he wheezed. "And I think you broke my nose. Is it bleeding?"

Raina's hand flew to her mouth. "I'm so sorry, honey. I didn't know it was you."

"I need an ice pack and a tranquilizer dart. Just put me out of my misery. You can apologize later," Matthew said through gritted teeth. His voice was tight with pain.

Raina grabbed his hand and helped him to the sofa. She flicked on a lamp. "You're not bleeding, but your nose is swollen. Do you want me to take a look at your groin?"

Matthew groaned and clutched his hands tighter between his legs. "Ice."

Raina grabbed the ice bucket on top of the coffee table. "I'll be back."

She ran to the ice machine down the hall. She felt cold and hot at the same time. Horrified at what she did and proud at the same time. She had taken on her fiancé and won. This was no small feat.

When Raina got back into the suite, Po Po was already up. There was a bottle of Tylenol on the coffee table next to a glass of water. Matthew was stretched out on the sofa with his eyes closed.

"He doesn't have a broken nose," Po Po said. "But he wouldn't let me examine his wee-wee."

Raina used the liner bag of the ice bucket to make an ice pack. She handed the bag of ice to Matthew with chagrin. "Well, at least we know Po Po's stun gun works."

Her grandma snorted in amusement. "So you took out your fiancé, huh?"

"How was I supposed to know it was him? I didn't want a repeat of what happened with Claire Boucher," Raina said.

Matthew's eyes flew open. "What happened with Claire?" His voice still sounded strained.

Raina told him everything that had happened since she last saw him—how Claire Boucher broke into her room, her dead body hidden in the laundry room, and what she found out about the suspects.

Matthew's eyes grew large with each new reveal. "Of course, she wouldn't catch a flight home or stay away from a murder," he mumbled under his breath.

Raina lowered herself to the ground until the two of them were at eye level. "What is going on? I thought you were supposed to help with a security upgrade, not get involved with stolen information from NASA."

Po Po leaned forward eagerly.

"I need a good night of sleep," Matthew said, giving Raina a pointed look. "We'll talk in the morning."

Raina sighed and gave Po Po a sideways glance. She wouldn't tell any secrets with her grandma nearby either, so she didn't blame him for his reluctance. "You better be here when I wake up in the morning. If you sneak off while I'm asleep, I might have to beat you again."

Po Po snickered.

Matthew closed his eyes and fell asleep before Raina had a chance to admonish him again. She tucked a blanket around him and clicked off the lamp directly over the sofa.

"Let's go to bed," Raina said to her grandma.

"Wow, you really beat him badly," Po Po whispered in awe. No one is going to recognize him with that swollen nose. And by tomorrow, he'll probably have a black eye."

Raina winced. She checked the time on her cell phone. It was two in the morning. "Goodnight."

She climbed into bed, throwing the covers over her head to signal she didn't want to chitchat. If given half a chance, her grandma would want a blow by blow of what happened. As Raina closed her eyes, a knot loosened in her chest, and she could take a deep breath for the first time. Matthew was back.

THE NEXT MORNING, Po Po lingered in her morning preparations, hoping to join in on the much-needed conversation between Raina and Matthew. Finally at eight thirty, Raina shooed her grandma out of the room.

While Matthew was in the shower, she fixed a simple breakfast for them: coffee, yogurt from the refrigerator, and a banana each. Without food in their systems, they might get into an argument over something silly.

When Matthew came out of the shower, Raina patted the seat next to her on the sofa. Instead of joining her, he leaned against the doorframe of the bathroom and crossed his arms. He gave her the police officer stare that probably would have made an innocent person confess to anything.

Raina raised an eyebrow. His nose was still red and angry looking. His left eye had darkened into a bruised ring. With a wig and the right clothes, he might be unrecognizable. "Let's eat first." She finished her last bite of yogurt and reached for a banana.

"Why didn't you go home?" Matthew said.

Raina wiggled the peeled banana. "I'm still eating. Come join me."

Matthew sighed and trudged over. When he reached for the cup of coffee, she averted her gaze to hide her smile. They ate in companionable silence for the next few minutes. At one point he reached across the sofa and patted Raina's thigh. She smiled at the gesture, knowing he had forgiven her for their late-night scuffle.

"Now that you had a good night of sleep and I fed you, it's your turn to tell me what's going on," Raina said. "Why did you disappear? And why did you try to sneak back in last night? If you had called, I wouldn't have to take such drastic measures."

"I trust you with my life, Rainy, but what I tell you

is strictly confidential. I can't have your grandma riding in like the Lone Ranger. Are we clear on this?"

She nodded.

"You're already halfway there with figuring out what's going on. Do you want to start and I'll fill in the blanks?"

Raina considered his words. She wondered if this was a trick question, but she loved the idea of presenting everything to him tied up in a neat bow. As silly as it sounded, she still wanted to impress her fiancé with her intellectual finesse.

"Okay, I'll start," she said. "You were hired to help with a security upgrade just like you told me, but I made the assumption it was for the hotel-casino. Now that I have more information, I know it's for NASA."

"There have been several security leaks over the past year," Matthew said. "They believed someone within the organization was stealing their top-secret research. Once they narrowed it down to a handful of people, they brought me in."

"But why you? I didn't know you had connections in NASA."

"I don't. A friend recommended me for the job. We were in the Marines together."

"And Claire Boucher and Gloria Tanaka are on your list of suspects?"

Matthew nodded. "Except at the time, we didn't know whether the two women were in cahoots with each other or if Gloria was a victim."

"Gloria came to the convention to confront Claire

about stealing her research from her unlocked computer—"

"Which shouldn't have happened in the first place. They were supposed to lock their computer anytime it was not in use," he said.

"There's not much you can do to combat carelessness. I'm assuming you had arranged to purchase the stolen information from Claire Boucher. And you were supposed to pick up the USB stick from her in the laundry room on the morning of her death."

He gave her a sharp look. "Yes, we intercepted her communications with the Russians. How did you find this out?"

"The video surveillance in the service hall. Now here's the part where you have to fill me in. I'm assuming Claire's death threw a monkey wrench into your plans. What have you been doing the last few days?"

"First, I had to figure out if Claire's death has anything to do with the Russians and national security," Matthew said.

"So you did leave town."

"Only for a day to do a debriefing. And once it was clear this was a plain old homicide case, the feds let me come back. They still want to get the USB stick. Claire said she had dropped it off with you?"

Raina explained what happened with Claire in their room and the location of the USB stick. She gave him a sheepish look. "It's because of her that I didn't hold back on you last night."

Matthew sighed. "It's just my luck," he muttered to himself. When he addressed Raina, he asked, "How did she know you were my fiancée?"

Raina frowned. "I thought you told her about me. I was trying to get tickets to the convention for Po Po. I wrote down my name and room number, and she commented on it. I thought she might have recognized my name because you told her about me."

Matthew shook his head. "I would never compromise your safety like that. Even though this security breach wasn't a dangerous assignment and all of it was a setup from the beginning, I would never put your name forward."

"You mean there is no super drone?"

Matthew gave her a sharp look. "Who helped you crack the password software?"

"Never you mind." Raina wasn't giving away her grandma's secret Science Ninja Club. "If the whole thing was a setup, could the Russians build a super drone with the stolen information?"

"Nope. They would spend time and money on something useless."

"What if Claire found out about the setup? I mean she could have a dossier on you, which linked us together."

Matthew sat back and thought about Raina's comment. "This theory would mean there is another player who knew about my involvement on the security breach and warned Claire.

"Gloria Tanaka?"

Matthew shook his head. "She's too low on the totem pole. She wouldn't have known about my involvement."

Raina thought about all the people she had met the last few days. She didn't know Willie's background, but it was unlikely she would have crossed paths with Matthew in the past. Hendricks was the muscle, and he didn't seem to have the capacity to do something so devious. There was only one person left. Matthew's old buddy from the Marines. "What about Lamar Stafford?"

Matthew blinked. "He recommended me to NASA. What makes you think he has anything to do with Claire's death?"

"I didn't say he has anything to do with her death. But I'm wondering if he told her about our relationship."

"Why would he compromise the security breach investigation?"

Raina raised an eyebrow. "So did you do anything to him in the past? Is he holding onto a grudge?"

Matthew groaned and closed his eyes. "I think I've been played."

14

KILL THE MESSENGER

After their conversation, Matthew closed his eyes and went back to sleep. The irritating man didn't explain his cryptic comment about Detective Stafford. He was probably still trying to process the situation.

Her fiancé was particular about doing things in sequential logical order. It was what made him such a good homicide detective by leaving no stone unturned. Until he reasoned things out, he played his cards close to the chest. While Raina liked to involve the entire village—his words—in her thought process.

As she had guessed, he had been taking catnaps in the hotel-casino, waiting for an opportunity to sneak back into their room without being noticed for the last two days. She had no idea if he would be in the room when she came back from breakfast, but she couldn't spend the morning waiting for him to wake up.

As she strode to the elevator, she felt a rising anger

toward Detective Lamar Stafford. If what Matthew said was correct, the entire gig was a setup to make him look bad? To what end? To never get another contract with the federal government? She wasn't sure what happened between the two men, but she was planning to find out.

Raina reached into her purse and pulled out the detective's business card. With Matthew in the picture, she didn't want to go headlong into this without running it by him. But if she ran things by him, then it sounded like she was asking for permission. This could set a bad precedent in their marriage.

The senior citizens greeted Raina with excitement. Since Claire Boucher's death was a plain old homicide and had nothing to do with national security, they could continue to investigate the case without treading on federal jurisdiction. For some reason, this reassured Raina. She might not know espionage, but she knew how to find the truth among suspects and murderers.

"Operation Photo Shoot was a failure," Po Po said. She hadn't touched her mushroom omelet. "We'll have to do better today."

Raina groaned inwardly. After the excitement of the previous evening, she had forgotten about the pool incident. "Maybe the Posse Club could look for Gloria Tanaka today. I still need to talk to her."

Po Po nodded. "It's your show, Sherlock. We are ready and able to do your bidding. The rest of the crew will have to start the operation without me." She winked exaggeratedly at Raina. "I need to pick up another costume. I think a friend of ours would like to be in disguise."

Raina took a sip of coffee. Geez, talk about being subtle. As long as Po Po said nothing about Matthew to the rest of the Posse Club, there was no harm in her grandma's antics. Though it seemed a tad cruel to not inform Maggie of her grandson's whereabouts, but that was his decision.

"Can we go over the suspects list again?" Frank asked. "I have forgotten some of the details." His eyes shifted from Raina to Po Po and back again as if to say he didn't entirely trust the details supplied by her grandma.

Raina held up her index finger. "First, there is Brian Anderson. His name badge was found outside in the loading dock area, which is right next to the crime scene. Ten thousand dollars is missing from the convention, and everyone blames Claire. He would have to make up for the shortfall the following year. Since this convention is his baby, he might be mad enough to get rid of her. And he had no alibi at the time of her death."

Frank nodded. "People have killed for less. And ten thousand dollars is a lot of money when you are trying to run a nonprofit."

Raina held up a second finger. "The other suspect is Gloria Tanaka. Claire got onto her computer at NASA and stole her research material." She paused, considering her next words. She couldn't go into the details that Matthew had given her, so she would have to pretend to guess at the truth. "I'm guessing that Claire planned to sell the stolen research, and Gloria came to the convention to get it back. If she doesn't recover the stolen research, she will lose her security clearance."

"This sounds like a stronger motive," Maggie said. "She's probably the killer maid."

"Also, Gloria seems to be having a good time since Claire's death," Po Po said.

Frank shook his head. "Or maybe she figured no one would find out about the stolen research, so she's not worried anymore. She could be an indirect benefactor rather than the murderer."

Raina nodded at Frank's words. "There could be some truth there, but I still need to talk with Gloria."

"What about Willie? I don't understand why she's making out with Brian and boinking Detective Stafford," Po Po said.

Raina cringed inwardly at her grandma's word choice. She didn't want that picture in her head. Willie was like a thick haze on this case. All smoke and mirrors.

"I think she's a distraction in this investigation. She has an alibi for the time of Claire's death. At first, I thought she might kill Claire for Brian. However, with Detective Stafford in the picture, there's no reason for her to kill Claire," Raina said. "And how did we go from holding hands to boinking?"

Po Po shrugged. "I would boink him."

Raina smacked her palm on her forehead. She didn't want that picture in her head either.

"Yeah, it's too bad I'm busy with someone else." Maggie leered at Frank. "Right, hon?"

Po Po covered her ears and closed her eyes. "No, no, no. I don't need to have that image in my head."

Raina snickered. Uh-huh. So her grandma finally got a taste of her own medicine.

Frank tapped the table with his fingers. "Can we get back on topic? What about this Detective Stafford? He is supposed to be investigating the crime, but we haven't heard a peep from him."

Raina addressed Maggie. "He claims to be Matthew's old buddy from the Marines. Said he spent holidays with you. Is there any truth to the story?"

Maggie was silent for a long moment as if running through her memory bank to search for the name. "I didn't get close enough to look at his face. From where I stood at the pool, he was a blur."

Po Po held up her cell phone. "He looks like this. A fine-looking man but he has no taste. He doesn't like cone bras, so I don't see a future for us."

Raina snorted coffee up the wrong windpipe and coughed. "Sorry. It went down the wrong way."

"I remember him," Maggie said. "He came once for Easter. I didn't think much of it because we didn't celebrate the day. Other than dying eggs for Matthew when he was a child, it wasn't on my radar."

"What's the nature of their friendship? Were they

good friends or were they more like co-workers?" Raina asked.

Maggie shook her head. "I don't know. I was just happy to have my grandson back, so I didn't care who he brought home."

Raina mulled over her conversation with Matthew for a moment. She put another bite of fluffy and buttery pancakes in her mouth. When she was done chewing, she looked up to see three sets of eyes watching her.

"Sorry, I needed brain food," Raina said, swallowing her bite. "I don't think Detective Stafford is a suspect. I think he's like Willie—a distraction. I know there's a lot happening here. There's Matthew, the convention, and other things, but they have nothing to do with Claire's death. We have to ignore them and follow through on the leads we do have. In this case, it's Brian Anderson and Gloria Tanaka."

The senior citizens were quick to agree with Raina's assessment of the situation. Either she was a better leader than she thought or the senior citizens didn't care and were along only for the ride.

Po Po paid the bill, and they stood to go their separate ways. Outside the diner, Maggie pulled Raina aside.

"I called and left a message with my son to let him know about my upcoming wedding." Maggie chewed her lower lip. "He lives in town."

Raina froze even as her mind raced at the implications. All this time, she had assumed no one knew the whereabouts of Matthew's father. Matthew would be devastated to know his father had been this close all along. "So he has been living here all these years?"

"No. It sounded like he moved here for health reasons last year. He didn't go into details."

"I don't know how Matthew will react if he sees his dad, but I know it won't be tears of joy."

"That's why I'm hoping you can prepare Matthew for this. It's my wedding, and I would like my only son to be there. I'm not picking him over my grandson." Maggie's voice broke, and her eyes filled with tears. "It would be nice to have my whole family with me for once."

Raina sighed. She hated being the messenger, but not helping her second grandma wasn't an option. The elderly lady had looked out for her during her childhood, she was her grandma's best friend, and her future grandma-in-law. "Okay, I'll try to soften him up."

RAINA STEPPED out of the elevator and turned the corner to find Willie standing in front of her suite. She dug into her purse, turning on the recording app on her phone and coming up with the key card for the room. At this stage in the investigation, she was probably making people nervous, even if they weren't suspects. It wouldn't hurt to have proof later on if something unexpected were to happen.

As Raina approached the general manager, her

hand tightened on the takeout bag of breakfast for Matthew. Even though her fiancé was still technically missing in action, and Willie had no reason to go into their room, Raina was still nervous. She had no idea if Matthew was still high on the suspects list for Claire's death, but since he was still in hiding, he probably feared he might be. And that fear mimicked the same one in Raina's heart.

All it took was one unlucky moment where Matthew stepped out before Raina got rid of Willie, and his cover would be blown. Though everything would eventually clear up, they didn't need Matthew detained until then. They still had a murder investigation to solve.

When Raina was within speaking distance, she called out, "Good morning, Willie. Are you here to talk about Brian Anderson?"

The tawny blonde scowled at Raina. Both hands rested on her waist. In her four-inch stilettos, she towered over Raina. "Did you have anything to do with the dunking I took at the pool yesterday?"

"No, were you in a swimsuit?" Raina asked, pretending to play dumb.

"I saw you at the pool yesterday. You were on the other side, hiding behind the palm tree with your wig and sunglasses on."

Raina decided to come clean. "Oh, all right. I was there because I thought you were meeting Brian. Imagine my surprise to find you holding hands with

Detective Stafford." Raina frowned. "Do they know you are dating both of them at the same time?"

"That's none of your business," Willie said through gritted teeth.

"You're right. It's none of my business." She glanced around the hallway, but they were alone. "Is that all you want to ask me?"

"I told Lamar what you said about Brian's name badge found outside in the loading dock area. He was surprised by the information." As Willie spoke, she leaned into Raina's personal space.

Raina stiffened, so she wouldn't take a step back. She felt like a child looking up at an authoritative adult about to give her a lecture.

"He is very interested in knowing how you got this information." Willie raised an eyebrow. "Don't make trouble for me because I will take you down."

"Is it your general policy to threaten the guests in your hotel-casino, Willie Machado?"

The general manager cocked her head as if assessing Raina's tone. "Of course not. I came to tell you the police had everything well in hand in this murder investigation. There is no reason for you to play Miss Fletcher while you're staying with us. If you see anything unusual, please report it to our security team."

Raina blinked at the change that came over Willie. Maybe Raina's use of the general manager's full name alerted her that something was amiss. "Is it a conflict of interest for Detective Stafford to take this case? Does his supervisor know that he is investigating a murder at his girlfriend's place of employment?"

Willie's jaw tightened. The vein at the base of her throat pulsed. "Lamar is interviewing people at the pool, and he wants to talk to you." She spun on her heels and marched toward the elevator. Her heels stabbed at the carpet with each step.

Raina shivered. Willie probably wouldn't mind stabbing Raina with those shoes. Luckily, looks couldn't kill.

15

OOOH-LA-LA!

When Raina stepped into the suite, Matthew was in the bathroom. She dropped the take-out bag on the coffee table and knocked on the door. "I got you more food."

Matthew came out—freshly showered and shaved—with a towel around his waist. Yum.

"Detective Stafford wants to chat with me. He's at the pool interviewing other people," Raina said.

Matthew gave her a lazy smile and curled a finger in her direction. "Lamar can wait."

Raina's stomach did a backflip, and she took a step toward him with a silly grin.

Before Raina could step into Matthew's embrace, Po Po burst into the room, waving a plastic bag. Her mouth dropped open at the sight of Matthew.

"Oooh-la-la. I can't believe I used to wipe your butt," Po Po said, openly staring.

Matthew flushed from head to toe. He jumped back into the bathroom and slammed the door.

Raina burst out laughing. "You're so bad. Why did you have to embarrass him?"

Po Po winked. "It keeps him on his toes. And besides, men should know what it feels like to be an object. We have suffered from their leering for generations. And now it's my turn to have a little revenge."

Raina shook a finger at her grandma. "Someday this will backfire on you. What's your escape plan when a man takes you up on the offer?"

Po Po shrugged. "Knee him in the ba—"

The bathroom door clicked open, and Matthew came out fully dressed. He kept his eyes on the carpet and edged around Po Po to sit on the sofa in the living room space. He tore into the take-out food like a hungry bear at a campsite, keeping his gaze fixed on a spot on the table.

Raina chuckled again. She didn't know her fiancé would embarrass this easily. She turned to her grandma. "What's in the bag?"

"Matthew's costume," Po Po said, pulling out the outfit. She held it up in front of her. "What do you think? And here's the wig." The hairpiece was long curly blond with a bright red bandana attached to it.

Raina's jaw dropped. The wig was even worse than her curly black hair. "No one would look at his face. They'll be too busy staring at the nest on top of his head. It ends halfway down his torso. Should we tie it back and braid it like Rapunzel's hair?"

Matthew sighed. "Even with the wig, my face is still recognizable."

Po Po shook the outfit. There was a denim jacket with a gazillion zippers and chains on it and denim cutoff shorts that were the male version of Daisy Dukes. "Not when you're wearing this. They'll be too busy staring at his hairy legs."

Raina bit her lower lip to keep the laughter from bursting out. "That's probably true. And in the surveillance video, the man last seen with Claire had a full facial beard. So if we stick blonde whiskers on your lips, it might be okay." Her fiancé would look like a street rat.

"I'm not going to the pool and chatting with Lamar Stafford in that outfit," Matthew said.

"Oh, come on. I went through several racks to find this for you," Po Po said. "Joanne Littleleaf wanted me to bring you to her booth. She wants a picture of you for her costume book."

"Hey, maybe you can even wear an eye patch," Raina said with a straight face.

Matthew gave her the stink eye. "Is that right?"

Matthew crumbled the takeout bag and tossed everything into the trash. He headed for the door. "See you guys later. Don't wait up for me."

"Wait!" Raina called out. "What's the game plan?"

Matthew gave her a blank stare. "What?"

"To catch Claire Boucher's murderer?" Raina said.

"Rainy, stay away from the murder investigation. That's Lamar's problem. I'm just here to deal with the

NASA security breach," Matthew said. He left the room without another word and closed the door behind him.

Raina stared at the door for a long moment. "I can't believe those words just came out of his mouth."

Po Po shook the costume again. "I wanted a picture of his hairy legs, so I can pass it around the police station when we get back home."

Raina gave her grandma a sideways glance. "Po Po, we're not compromising Matthew's authority in the community by passing around embarrassing photos of him. His authority keeps him safe when he's out and about doing his job."

Po Po harrumphed. She packed the costume back into the bag. "I guess you're right." She muttered to herself, "But it sure would be fun to see."

As her grandma stashed the costume into the corner of her closet, Raina opened the door. "Come on. We'll have to hurry if we don't want to miss the action by the pool."

Po Po stepped out, and they trotted to the elevator. "I almost forgot. I was digging through the box of wigs when I found a black T-shirt with the hotel's logo on it."

Raina tapped the call button for the elevator. "Maybe someone left it behind?"

Po Po raised an eyebrow. "Rainy, you know better. There's no such thing as a coincidence when it comes to murder."

"Joanne is such a gentle soul," Raina said even though her mind was already running through their conversations, looking for clues. She told her grandma her last conversation with Joanne about their financial woes.

"Like Gloria Tanaka, this is their livelihood at stake," Po Po said. "Her motive is equally as strong. And like Brian, they have been coming to the convention for years, so it would be easy to find out about the maid's schedule."

"If we find out who stole Claire's phone, we might have the killer," Raina said, stepping into the elevator car. "But that's not likely to happen, so we need to lure the killer out of hiding and into doing something drastic."

"Matthew will not like this," Po Po said.

Raina shrugged. "I didn't like him telling me to mind my own business either."

"I don't understand why he is confronting Detective Stafford," Po Po said. "Isn't Matthew a suspect?"

"He's counting on their years of"—Raina made air quotes with her fingers—"friendship to get answers about the NASA gig."

Po Po raised an eyebrow. "What if the friendship was all one-sided?"

"I'm afraid of that too."

RAINA and her grandma got out of the elevator and power walked to the rooftop pool. Every patio and lounge chair had someone on it even though it was already eighty degrees. With sunglasses and an iced drink, it probably was perfect sunbathing weather. The heat radiated off the concrete and tile, and Raina squinted against the glare.

"Over there," Po Po said, pointing to their left.

Raina's gaze swept across the patio area to the bar. Detective Stafford in a white blazer and blue jeans leaned forward as he chatted earnestly with Matthew. The next thing she knew Detective Stafford reached into his back pocket, pulled out a pair of handcuffs, and snapped them around Matthew's wrists.

Raina sucked in a deep breath ready to scream and barely managed to stifle it the last moment. She ran over to the Watering Hole bar with her grandma hot on her heels. "What's going on here? Why are you arresting Matthew?" She tried getting between Detective Stafford and Matthew, but they ignored her.

The two men were in a staring contest where no one else existed for them. There was an undercurrent that Raina didn't understand. Was this just regular male posturing or something more?

A uniformed officer came around the bar to join them. "Is the suspect ready for the trip to the station?"

While Detective Stafford conferred with the officer, Matthew leaned down to whisper in Raina's ear in Chinese. "Do what you do best. I love you."

"What does that mean? Do I need to get you a lawyer?" Raina replied in Chinese.

Matthew shook his head. "Just stay out of trouble. It will all turn out fine."

"Will you be back by Tuesday? You should be there for your grandma's wedding."

Matthew's eyes widened. "Ah Ma? Who is she marrying?"

Raina cringed inwardly. She didn't mean to break the news to him like this, but it just slipped out. "Frank Small."

"Let's go," the officer said, holding onto Matthew's forearm to lead him away.

Matthew resisted for a moment. "Please stop the wedding." He followed the officer toward the elevator.

As Raina watched her fiancé disappear, she swallowed her rising panic. She didn't know how things were done in Las Vegas, but she doubted they could frame Matthew on a murder charge. And since he had seen worse things than a jail cell in his lifetime, she knew he would be fine.

This didn't mean she wasn't upset, especially with his plea for Raina to stop his grandma's wedding. She hoped he only needed time to process the information. There was no way she would ruin Maggie's future happiness to indulge her fiancé.

Raina spun around and pointed a finger at Detective Stafford. "I thought you said he was your friend."

Detective Stafford held up the palms of his hands. "I'm just doing my job. He has been dodging us for the last few days. He confessed that he was the man with the beard and baseball cap who met Claire Boucher in the laundry room. It is my job to bring him down to the station for further questioning. It doesn't matter if we're best friends or enemies."

"How did Claire know about my relationship with Matthew? Did you tell her this?"

"No. The only time I mentioned your relationship was to Willie Machado."

Raina considered his words. And Willie must have mentioned Raina's relationship with Matthew to Brian Anderson. So if Brian mentioned this tidbit of gossip to Claire, did this mean they were friends even though they had their disagreement over the breakfast spread? This could change Brian's role in this murder investigation.

"Are you aware that Willie is also seeing another man?" The words sounded mean and petty to Raina's ears, but she couldn't help herself.

Detective Stafford blinked. "I'm not sure why this is your business, but yes, I know about Brian Anderson. Willie and I are not exclusive."

"Then shouldn't you excuse yourself from this case? There's a lot of conflicts of interest here. First, there is your relationship with Willie. And second, there is your supposed friendship with Matthew. I don't understand why you would recommend him for the NASA gig if you were planning to betray him."

Detective Stafford's eyes widened. "Whoa! I didn't betray Matthew. When we spoke a few months ago, he mentioned wanting to elope with you. When this gig came up, I thought it would be perfect for him. He gets to come to Vegas with you, do this little job, and walk away with several thousand dollars. It was supposed to be an easy job."

"You two are really friends?" Raina flushed as the words came out of her mouth. She sounded like a paranoid bimbolina.

"Yeah. I told you—Matthew saved my life."

Raina's face grew even redder. She knew Matthew so well she assumed he would tell her the important details of his time away from her. "I'm sorry. He never mentioned you, so it should be understandable why I am suspicious."

"No harm done, but I have to get to back to the station." Detective Stafford tried to step around Raina.

"Wait! Is Matthew under arrest for Claire Boucher's murder?"

"No. He wants to go to the station for questioning."

"I don't understand. Why does he have to leave in handcuffs? Should I get him a lawyer?"

Detective Stafford shrugged. "The handcuffs were his idea. As to the lawyer, I don't know. You of all people should know what he's up to."

As Raina watched Detective Stafford leave, her gaze shifted around the poolside patio. If their friendship was real, then this public arrest must be a charade. A move to force something to happen. Why didn't her fiancé trust Raina enough to let her in on the game?

"What do we do now, Sherlock?" Po Po said anxiously. "Do we tell Maggie what happened?"

"I don't know anything anymore," Raina whispered.

She swallowed the lump in her throat. For days there had been this nagging worry about Matthew's whereabouts. And when he finally showed up, she had assumed they would work on the Claire Boucher case together and clear up the mess at NASA like an unstoppable dynamic duo. They hadn't even gotten off the bench yet, and they were already sidelined.

Was this a temporary setback or something worse? What if her normally capable fiancé couldn't get himself out of this mess? It would explain why he admitted he was the bearded man in the surveillance video. After all, the law was more lenient on those who turned themselves in.

"You ladies want a drink?" the bartender said, approaching them.

Raina got onto the empty stool next to the bar. "Can I get ice coffee here?"

The bartender pointed to one of those instant coffee machines. "I can pour it over ice."

"Good enough for me," Raina said.

"A whiskey sour for me," her grandma said.

Raina raised her eyebrow.

"Desperate times call for desperate measures. Besides, I'm too old to care what people think," Po Po said, settling onto her stool.

The bartender went off to make their drinks. The two of them sat in companionable silence. Raina's mind whirled and went over her conversation with Matthew. She didn't understand his last words. What she did best was to ask nosy questions and somehow stumble on the truth. Surely he didn't want her to continue a murder investigation?

Raina paid the bartender and sipped her coffee. It wasn't good, but it would have to do, especially since she paid five dollars for it. As she relaxed the anxiety clutching at her heart, she knew what she had to do. It was not in her nature to sit and wait for something to work itself out. Right or wrong she was a woman of action, and Matthew knew this.

"I need to talk to Brian Anderson. Maybe now that the"—Raina made air quotes with her fingers—"the real murderer is caught, he might talk to me."

Po Po gave Raina a doubtful look. "Why would he talk now?"

"If he doesn't, I'll complain to corporate about Willie's behavior."

"And you think he will want to keep his girlfriend out of trouble?"

"Yes, because only a man desperately in love would be willing to share his girlfriend with someone else."

Raina sounded more confident than she felt, though her intuition said she was on the right track. After all, everyone had a weak point—she just had to figure what would make Brian squeal.

16

AN UNHOLY ALLIANCE

As Raina finished her coffee, Po Po's hands flew across her cell phone screen, tapping out a message to the rest of the Posse Club. They were to synchronize their watches and rendezvous in front of the main hall in fifteen minutes. Raina left the Posse Club to plan their search of the suspects. Since they promised not to engage the suspects on their own, Raina didn't see any harm in letting them feel like they were part of the investigation.

Raina made her way upstairs to the security headquarters. She was hoping Hendricks would help her search for Brian or Gloria through their security system. Barring this, maybe he could find their room numbers for her. The last time they had spoken, Hendricks sounded agreeable to a partnership between them, especially if he were to get the credit for the takedown.

The pregnant security guard met her at the door again. She blocked the entrance with her body. "Is the boss expecting you?"

Raina smiled, hoping she looked non-threatening. With her height and her hair, who would believe she was dangerous? Delusion maybe. "No, but he will talk to me. Let him know that Raina Sun is here."

"All right. Just wait a minute."

The security guard closed the door, leaving Raina to twiddle her thumbs for the next few minutes. She briefly contemplated making faces at the security camera pointing down at her.

The door opened shortly again, but this time it was Hendricks. He stepped out into the hallway and closed the door behind him. "What is it? Do you have information for me?"

His tank of a body blocked Raina from the camera. His eyes were hooded, and his square jaw was clenched. But his hand tapped against his thigh like he was trying to get rid of excess energy.

"I need to talk to Brian Anderson or Gloria Tanaka. However, I am having a hard time tracking them down between the various conference rooms, the shopping areas, and the casino floor. Can you find them on your surveillance cameras for me?" Raina said.

Hendricks hesitated as if debating the merits of getting involved in what could be a harebrained scheme.

"I promise it will be worth your while. As soon as I

talk to them, I will have a lead on this murder investigation. I promise," Raina said.

The temptation must have been too strong for Hendricks to resist. He led her back inside to the command center and told his staff what Raina needed.

"But we don't even know what they look like, boss," the pregnant woman said.

Raina pulled out her cell phone from her purse. "I have pictures of them." She tapped on the photo app and held out the phone to show the images to Hendricks and his staff.

"Is it legal to take pictures of people like this?" the pregnant woman said.

Raina shrugged. The pictures from Po Po's hidden camera probably fell in a gray area. "They were out in public places. If they didn't want their picture taken as part of the background, they could walk around with a bag over their faces."

The pregnant woman harrumphed and turned back to her screens. Her coworker was already buzzing through the video feeds in front of him. It took about five minutes before they finally located Brian Anderson heading to the laundry room of all places.

"I guess it's true. The murderer always goes back to the scene of the crime," Hendricks said, studying the live video footage. "Come on. Let's go have a chat with him."

Hendricks led Raina to the service elevator at the end of the hall. It was twice as wide as the regular elevator. Instead of wood paneling and mirrors inside the car, it was plain stainless steel. Functional and no frills.

"Can you wait in the service hall? I want to speak to Brian alone first," Raina said.

Hendricks shook his head. "What if he was the killer? He would snap you like a twig. No offense, but you're a lightweight."

Raina bit back a sarcastic reply. She didn't want to start their partnership with bickering like school children. "But I can scream really loud."

"Yeah, you look like a screamer."

It took all of Raina's willpower to keep from rolling her eyes. "Can't you run in real quick? It's less intimidating for me to question Brian than for you to do it. You're a formidable man."

Hendricks puffed out his chest at the compliment. "I guess you're right. We wouldn't want the pip-squeak to pee in his pants. I'll wait for you outside."

They stepped out at the service elevator and split up. Hendricks strolled over to the storage room and went inside, leaving the door ajar. Raina stood in front of the laundry room, blocking the only exit. The ventilation in the room was horrendous because moisture clung to the air. Raina felt her hair fuzzing at the humidity. Great. She probably looked like the bride of Frankenstein.

All the industrial machines were in various stages of washing and drying. There was the swoosh of water hitting the drum, the slapping of linens and towels against each other, and the whirling dryer. Raina hoped the maids working in the laundry room were wearing earplugs. Prolonged exposure to noise of this level could lead to hearing loss. Maybe this was why the head housekeeper rotated the laundry chore among all the maids.

Brian turned away from the maid and stiffened at the sight of Raina.

"You! What are you doing here?" Brian said, holding his laundry bag in front of him as if it were a talisman to ward off unwanted nosy people.

Raina smiled, hoping she looked friendly instead of like the Big Bad Wolf. She had to strain to hear what he said. "I came to pick up my costume. Hey, have you heard the news about Claire Boucher's killer?"

Brian did a double take, opening his mouth like he wanted to say something, but no words came out. With his poorly placed toupee and bushy sideburns, he looked like a blowfish in skinny black jeans.

Raina smiled inwardly at the hook she threw out. She gestured for Brian to follow her and led him to the storage room in the service hall. The noise was muffled enough to hold a conversation without shouting.

"How did they catch him?" Brian asked.

"How do you know the killer was a man?" Raina asked.

Brian glanced up and down the hall, patting his toupee. The hairpiece shifted from the attention. If touching his hair was Brian's nervous tick, someone should tell him to stop.

Raina watched the gesture with amusement and wondered if the toupee might slip off. The silence stretched until Raina couldn't stand it any longer.

"Let me guess. You were outside in the loading dock area when Claire was in here. That was how you lost your name badge." She paused, watching for the impact of her speech.

Brian clenched his jaw, holding back his words.

"And you saw someone leave from the side entrance," Raina continued. "You were a witness."

"I don't want any trouble."

"Why would you be in trouble? You didn't kill Claire."

"I don't want to get involved. I have trouble enough of my own."

"But it's your civic duty to help the police. Don't you want the police to capture Claire's killer? We can't have a murderer roaming the streets."

"You don't understand."

"Then explain it to me. I'm a good listener," Raina whispered, using her most soothing tone.

"I was good friends with Claire's husband. They used to come every year to the Rock and Jam Convention. When her husband died, we still kept in touch with the occasional Christmas card. And two years ago, Claire finally started coming back."

"And when she asked you to be her lookout, you agreed," Raina guessed.

"Claire has several patents outside of her work with NASA. She was meeting a potential buyer for one of her patents, but she didn't trust the person. So she wanted me close by in case the man tried to steal her prototype. I didn't see this prototype, so I assumed it was small enough to fit inside her purse."

Raina raised an eyebrow. Either Brian was a chump, or he was lying. "And you just said yes?"

"I had no reason to say no. What kind of man would I be if I didn't help my friend's widow?"

"But why were you outside? I don't see how you could help if you weren't even within shouting distance."

"I could see through the glass panel with binoculars. When the Asian man came out, I stepped into the hedges to hide from him. I must have lost my badge then."

"After the Asian man left, you didn't check on Claire," Raina said. If he did, he would have shown up on the surveillance video or run into the killer maid. "If you had gone to check on her, you might have been able to save her."

"It's not my fault." Brian's voice came out in a squeak.

"Did Claire tell you anything else about the man she was meeting?" Raina asked, changing the subject. Now that Brian seemed emotionally vulnerable, it was time to press him for answers.

"I don't know anything about the deal. But while I stood outside waiting for her, I realized I had made a mistake. I didn't feel comfortable with the situation at all. If the sale was on the up and up, why would she need to meet the buyer in the laundry room?"

Raina didn't have an answer to his question. "Why did she ask you? She didn't know anyone else at the convention?"

"I don't know why. Maybe because we've known each other for a long time."

"Why didn't you check the laundry room?"

"I didn't see her with the binoculars. I even waited, so I assumed that I missed her when I was hiding in the hedges. I went around the front of the hotel-casino to join the convention again. As soon as I got there, people came up asking me questions, and I completely forgot about her."

"When did you find out about her death?" Raina asked.

"After lunch. I was shocked."

"Weren't you upset with her for stealing the ten thousand dollars?"

Brian stared at Raina like she grew another head. "Yeah, but I didn't want her to die."

Raina cocked her head and studied Brian for a long moment. His anguish seemed real enough, but there was an undercurrent of another emotion. "Do you feel guilty?"

Brian shifted from foot to foot. "Um, about what?"

Raina zeroed in on his tone. Did he sound evasive? He didn't appear to be talking about survivor's guilt.

"About the money?" As soon as the words were out of her mouth, Raina knew she was on the right track.

Brian continued to avoid her gaze. "I have no idea how much Claire was supposed to get for selling a patent."

Raina narrowed her eyes, willing him to look at her. She hardened her voice. "I'm not talking about Claire's patent deal. I'm talking about the missing ten thousand dollars. You embezzled the money and let Claire take the fall for it."

Brian finally met her eyes. He had turned ashen like the underside of a dead fish. "She was already dead. It wasn't like the board members could do anything to her now. I planned to put the money back..."

"I bet you took the money before you were hospitalized."

"Please don't say anything. I just need time to pay it back."

Raina gave him a deadpan stare. If she hadn't guessed correctly, would he volunteer to return the loot? "What did you spend the money on? Or maybe who did you spend the money on? Willie?"

Brian hung his head, and his toupee slipped forward. "You can't blame me for dreaming. A woman like Willie would never look twice at someone like me without the money." He gestured at his stoop-shouldered frame.

His assessment of the situation was probably right.

Already in his late forties, with what her grandma would call a flat backside and zero muscle tone, he was scant competition for Detective Stafford.

"Once the money runs out, she'll probably walk out too," Raina said.

"But at least I got the girl for once."

At the look of anguish on Brian's face, Raina didn't have the heart to press him further. She could ask more questions about his relationship with Willie, but it was none of her business. And if Brian had no idea Willie was seeing somebody else, Raina didn't have the heart to tell him.

As Brian stepped through the double swinging doors, Hendricks came out of the storage room to stand beside Raina.

"Did you hear the conversation?" she asked.

"Every pathetic word," Hendricks said.

"What do you think? Do you believe him?"

"I don't see why he would lie. Not after his confession of stealing the money." Hendricks's face twisted into a sneer. "Some men just have to pay to get laid. I'm glad I never have that problem."

Raina grimaced inwardly. Why did some men always feel the need to brag about their sexual conquests?

"And he mentioned the Asian man who got arrested. Brian would have to be outside to see this," Hendricks said.

Raina nodded in agreement. She wasn't surprised Hendricks knew of Matthew's arrest earlier, but she was surprised he didn't insist the police already got the killer. Maybe he had more faith in her than she realized. "Can your staff find Gloria Tanaka for us?"

Hendricks pulled out his cell phone. "They can try."

17

PACKING IT UP

Raina and Hendricks cooled their heels while the security team looked for Gloria Tanaka in the surveillance videos. The maid came out once to go across to the storage room and went back into the laundry room, giving them covert glances.

Hendricks stepped outside into the loading dock to take a call.

Raina pulled out her cell phone, but there weren't any messages. The battery bar on her phone was at thirty percent. With the excitement of last night, she had forgotten to plug in her phone. Should she call or text Matthew? With the morning traffic, he probably hadn't even arrived at the police station yet. Maybe she should wait until after lunch. She might have time to run upstairs to charge her phone. She would hate to cut their call short because of a dead battery.

She texted the Posse Club. With Hendricks and his

team helping to locate Gloria, she didn't expect the senior citizens to do more than pretend to be detectives.

I'VE TALKED TO BRIAN. HE'S NOT OUR KILLER.

Maggie replied back.

OKAY. WE'RE IN THE EXHIBIT HALL, HELPING YOUR GRANDMA SNEAK INTO THE BACK OF EACH BOOTH. SHE THINKS THE KILLER HID THE DISGUISE DOWN HERE.

Raina blinked at the message. She didn't know what her grandma thought the killer would hide at such a public place, but maybe that was the point. Criminals had been known to hide things in plain sight. In this case, would it be the maid disguise?

She made a mental note to circle back to have a chat with Joanne Littleleaf. Her grandma had mentioned finding a maid T-shirt among the box of wigs. Could the killer have discarded pieces of his or her disguise among the booths? That would be a smart thing to do. If Joanne was the killer maid, she would be stupid to hide the evidence in her own booth. And the saleswoman was anything but stupid.

Raina replied back to Maggie.

KEEP A TIGHT REIN ON PO PO. ASK FRANK TO RESTRAIN HER IF SHE DOES ANYTHING STUPID.

Maggie's answer was almost immediate.

THEN WE NEED TO LOCK HER IN A PADDED CELL!

Raina chuckled at the message. This sounded about right. Po Po had spent most of her youth being an obedient Chinese wife. By the time Raina's mom had moved home with her three children, her grandma threw off the yoke of conformity and became this new and improved version, reliving a second childhood. While it could be trying at times, Raina wouldn't have things any other way.

Hendricks came through the side exit, interrupting Raina's wandering thoughts. He held up his cell phone. "They found Gloria. She's at the buffet."

They trotted toward the casino floor. Hendricks pushed open the double swinging door and held it for her.

"Thank you," Raina said, stepping through. "Is Gloria by herself?"

"She's with some dude with long dreadlocks. I'm telling you, this convention always brings out the weirdos."

"Gloria is a NASA researcher."

"That's even worse. Those types are always so uptight in their everyday life. When they come here, they think it's like Woodstock or something. My boss is a prime example of this. She trades in her pants suit to run around in a skimpy dress with half her ass hanging out and an ugly wig."

Raina gave Hendricks a sideways glance. Boy, did he sound bitter. "What's your problem? Are you upset because you don't get to join the fun?"

"I get to spend all week telling couples to go get a room—literally. Then I gotta turn a blind eye on the drugs unless it gets out of hand. And housekeeping is moaning about all the puke and mess they have to clean up. Trust me, lady, you don't want to be on the staff this week."

Raina never considered how the people who worked here felt about the convention. "Some people might call this heaven."

Hendricks grunted. "Some heaven."

"Look on the bright side. With the murder, they might not come back again next year."

"Or it might grow bigger, which seems to be the case every year."

By this time, they were at the buffet line, and Hendricks stopped his complaints. He used his tank of a body to get to the head of the line. Raina followed on his heels. When people protested, he growled out, "Security," and they gave way uneasily.

"She's sitting in a booth next to the restroom," Hendricks said, striding ahead.

Raina trotted to keep up with his much longer legs. She probably looked ridiculous like a high-spirited puppy keeping up with a foxhound in a chase.

Hendricks got to the booth first. From the way he was frowning, Raina knew it wasn't good news even before she got there. The booth was empty with no sign that Gloria would return with more food. The used plates with half-eaten food were still on the table with crumpled napkins on top of them. The receipt was turned upside down, indicating the previous occupants were done eating.

"I guess we're back to square one," Hendricks said. "Do you want to hang out here while I ask my staff to look for her again?"

"No. Why don't you call me when you hear something? There's someone else I would like to talk to," Raina said, thinking of Joanne Littleleaf.

She also didn't like her grandma snooping around the exhibit hall without supervision. The members of the Posse Club were more likely to egg her grandma on than to urge caution. Senior citizens with free time on their hands and a *c'est la vie* attitude were a horrible combination for mischief.

Hendricks narrowed his eyes suspiciously. "What are you planning to do? Our deal was for me to take down the killer."

Raina gave him a deadpan stare. For someone who was the head of security, he had more faith in an amateur sleuth than himself for cracking the case. She didn't know whether to be flattered or to be worried about this partnership with him. After all, she was counting on Hendricks's muscle to keep her from physical harm.

"Yes, I remember our bargain, but I need to check on my grandma. You know how she is," Raina said.

Hendricks rolled his eyes. "Oh, I remember your

grandma, all right. I'm just thankful my granny was nothing like yours."

Raina was offended by his comment, but she kept a neutral expression. Her fun-loving grandma was the epitome of love and generosity. So what if she had eccentric characteristics? She was never ill-mannered or vulgar.

Instead of replying with a snide comment about removing the stick from his bum, Raina rattled off her cell phone number. They agreed to check in with each other later.

As Raina left the buffet, she wondered if Hendricks would try to confront Gloria without her, thereby cutting off Raina's role in the murder investigation. He could play big man on campus for all she cared, but she didn't want him to tip Gloria off. The NASA scientist moved about the convention like a sly cat already, and she wasn't even trying to evade them. How much more difficult would it be if she tried?

Raina pulled out her cell and texted the Posse Club.

I'M GOING TO THE EXHIBIT HALL.

Po Po replied back.

WE'RE IN THE MAIN HALL, WAITING FOR OUR TURN ON THE STAGE.

Raina frowned at the message. When did the three of them learn to perform rock music?

Even if they rented the instruments, wouldn't they need time to practice before a live stage? At least this would keep the three senior citizens from getting in trouble. She replied back.

Have fun.

Raina strode into the exhibit hall and made a beeline for Joanne Littleleaf's costume booth. The vinyl banner with the business name was taken down. Only half the merchandise was still on the racks. Boxes were all over the small twelve by twelve space, some closed and taped up and others halfway full. She frowned. Were they in the middle of packing up? The convention wasn't scheduled to end for another day.

Instead of Joanne Littleleaf in the booth, a Native American man was taping up a cardboard box. His skin was brown and weathered—an outdoorsy type. Though his hair was completely white, he still moved with the energy and vigor of a much younger man.

"Hi, are you Joanne's husband?" Raina asked.

He glanced up from his task. "Yes, ma'am. My name is John Littleleaf."

"My name is Raina Sun. I met your wife a few days ago when we bought several costumes from her. I was hoping to catch her before she leaves. I thought you would be here for the entire convention."

"Our eldest fell off a ladder. We have to get home to help with the grandkids."

"Oh, no. Is he all right?"

"I don't know. It sounds like he got banged up bad."

"I hope he makes a speedy recovery." Raina hesitated. It would sound callous to broach the subject of the murder investigation at the moment. "Do you need a hand?" She stepped into the booth and grabbed a costume off the racks. "Which box does this go into?"

"No, I can't have you help me," John said.

"I don't mind at all. If your wife were here, I would do the same thing. I like being helpful." And often people felt obligated to talk with helpful people.

John gestured at a box to Raina's right. "The boxes are labeled by costume types. Just put all the sizes for a particular costume together."

Raina studied the labels. Western, superhero, rock, and a few others. She hadn't noticed the other type of costumes the first time she was here. She had been too busy pumping Joanne for information. "Do you have an online store? Some of these costumes have fantastic details."

John finished taping the box and stacked it on top of the other closed boxes at the rear of the booth. "Not us. We do it the old-fashioned way by going from show to show. Our other son maintains the online shop for us. He packages and ships from our garage. It's getting harder to make a living with the competition online. Every other customer shows us a lower online price with their cell phones. The fabric these online sites use is cheap plastic that lasts for one or two wearings." He droned for several minutes on how technology had changed their livelihood.

Raina didn't have the heart to mention that technology had disrupted every industry. When he paused for breath, she asked, "Were you able to make a profit from this year's show? Joanne was worried about this when we last spoke."

John hesitated. "So how long have you known Joanne?"

"Just a few days."

"And she told you all this?"

Raina shrugged, pretending a nonchalance she didn't feel. He must wonder why his wife would confide to a virtual stranger. "You know how it is with women. When we get together, we chat about everything." She hoped he would take her explanation at face value.

John rolled his eyes. "Yeah, I know how she is." He got another box and started filling it. "With the cost of gas and the increased fees, we lost money this year. We might break even if we stay another day, but our son needs us."

Raina winced. "I'm sorry. With the holidays just around the corner, this must come as another blow."

"We'll get by. We have some savings."

"She made it sound like you guys would lose the house if you don't make a profit."

John chuckled. "We inherited the farm from my family. If worse comes to worst, the vegetable garden and the chickens will keep us fed. It's not like we'll eat cat food in our golden years."

"Oh."

John gave Raina a sideways glance. "Maybe she was trying to get you to spend more money."

Raina's jaw dropped. Had Joanne played her for a fool? "You're kidding me. She has done this before?"

John lost the amusement on his face. "I'm sorry. I don't mean for it to come out like this. Joanne doesn't do this intentionally. She came from a poor family, so she's always worried about becoming a bag lady. It's just how she's wired."

As Raina folded the costumes into the box in front of her, she thought about their conversation. If what John said was true, then Joanne Littleleaf would have no motive for killing Claire Boucher in a fit of anger. And yes, their livelihood might be threatened, but according to her husband, they still had their house, their toy hauler, and their merchandise. Plenty to keep them going for a while.

"John, my grandma found a hotel maid shirt in the wig box yesterday. You might want to take that out before you pack it up," Raina said.

John went over to the wig box, rifled through the contents, and pulled out a black T-shirt. He frowned. "I wonder how this got in here?"

Raina watched his expression carefully, and he looked genuinely puzzled. He held the shirt up by pinching it with his thumb and index finger.

"It doesn't belong to you guys?" Raina asked.

John shook his head. "Why would we want a hotel T-shirt?" He glanced at the tag. "It's a medium. Joanne and I haven't fit into a medium since 1980." He set it on the floor next to a half-full trash bag.

"How do you think it got there?" Raina asked. She hoped she sounded curious instead of probing.

John gestured at the blue tarp surrounding their booth. "This isn't a secured storage unit. They lock the main entrance when the exhibit hall is closed, but anyone with the key can probably get in here." His expression changed, going from puzzlement to disgust.

"Are you okay? What is it?" Raina asked, leaning forward. Did he remember something?

"I'm grossed out by a thought. What if a maid came in here with a boyfriend for some hanky panky? I would have to disinfect everything when we get home."

Raina burst out laughing. This was the kind of comment her grandma would make. "There isn't any horizontal surface in here. Maybe they were on the floor."

John shuddered. "Now I didn't need that image in my head, young lady."

"Do you mind if I keep the maid T-shirt?" Raina asked.

"Sure, go right ahead."

Raina put the T-shirt in a plastic bag and stuffed it into her purse. She had a feeling the shirt might belong to the killer maid. It was better to be cautious than to lose this piece of evidence. Detective Stafford might want to see it.

When she left the booth half an hour later, she was convinced the Littleleafs probably had nothing to do with the murder. After all, the net loss from the convention couldn't be more than a few thousand dollars. And yes, people have killed for less, but those murderers were often desperate for the money. In this case, and with John's steadiness, she knew the Littleleafs would weather through the loss. It might be a challenging year, but it wouldn't be a year that would crush them.

She pulled out her notebook and crossed Joanne from her list of suspects. She jotted down the notes from her conversation with John and stared for a long moment at the remaining name on the list. Gloria Tanaka.

Her instinct had been right all along—this case circled back to Matthew's side gig. And with her fiancé still at the police station and probably spending the night in a holding cell, this left Raina to prove his innocence. She felt vindicated for her involvement in the investigation.

18

A VICTORY

Raina strolled to the café to pick up a sandwich and an iced coffee for lunch. The lack of sleep from the night before finally caught up with her and a wave of exhaustion hit her. While she waited for her order, she texted the Posse Club, letting them know her plan to eat in her room and take a short nap. Until someone called on the whereabouts of Gloria, Raina didn't have anything better to do. She had already spoken with the other suspects and ruled them out.

She texted Matthew, but he didn't reply. This was no surprise. Police business cranked at a snail's pace, where the same questions were posed in multiple ways to drag out the details from both witnesses and suspects alike.

Once in the suite, Raina ate like a starving bear who just woke up from hibernation. It was close to two in the afternoon. The lettuce was wilted and the tomato runny on the tuna sandwich. She tossed out the tomato and wiped off the excessive tomato juice and mayonnaise. She took a slow sip of coffee and hummed in contentment. Now this was heavenly. Creamy and sweet without an acid aftertaste. Yum.

Raina set the alarm clock for thirty minutes and grabbed the plastic bag with the maid T-shirt from her purse. Having something from a murderer next to the bed was probably bad luck. She hid the plastic bag inside the closet, behind the suitcases. She returned to the bed, slipped off her shoes and jeans, and crawled in. She was out before her head hit the pillow.

When the hair on her arms stiffened, she became conscious. The gooseflesh sensation was so at odds with the warm cocoon of the comforter that she woke in confusion for half a heartbeat. A thread of tension ran through her, but she couldn't figure out why. The room was dim from the drawn curtains. Why would she feel the need to flee in bed? Was this the remnant of a bad dream?

Something rustled.

Raina's eyes flew open. Who was in the room? She squinted at the dim light and scanned the room. She could just make out the outline of someone sitting on the sofa. And this person wasn't her grandma.

She jerked upright in the bed, automatically reaching for the purse she had left on the side table. Her hands patted around the surface and came up with nothing. She froze. Where was her purse with her pepper spray and stun gun?

The stranger clicked on the lamp next to the sofa.

Raina averted her face at the sudden brightness. When her eyes adjusted to the light, she gasped. The suspect she had been trying to track down all morning was in her room—Gloria Tanaka.

"How did you get in here?" Raina asked. Her voice was raspy like she needed a drink of water. She cleared her throat. "Are you planning to kill me?"

"I'm a rocket scientist. A hotel lock isn't much of a challenge for me," Gloria said.

Raina noticed Gloria didn't reply to her other question. "How did you find my room?"

"I followed you up from the café. It wasn't hard to find you. Not many Asians have hair like yours."

Raina smoothed her hair self-consciously. It probably looked a fright after being mashed up by the pillow. As soon as the thought flittered through her mind, she dismissed it. She shouldn't think about her hair at a moment like this.

"You didn't answer my second question," Raina said, praying to her ancestors that she wasn't pushing her luck. Without a weapon of any kind, all she had left was her bravado. Maybe she could talk herself out of this mess. "Are you planning to kill me?"

"Why would I want to kill you?" Gloria asked, her eyes twinkling with amusement.

This was the first time Raina got a good look at Gloria. She was probably somewhere in her late thirties to her early forties. Her hair was still a jet black, and her face unlined. Her brown almond-shaped eyes watched Raina like she was a specimen in a lab tube. It made Raina's skin crawl.

The two of them were evenly matched physically, though Raina was about ten years younger. She hoped youth and exercise would give her an edge against someone who sat in an office chair all day.

"Because most people don't come inside someone's hotel room without knocking or watch the person sleep," Raina said.

Gloria appeared to consider the comment. "I'm not good with interpreting people's body language, but you seem tense."

Raina blinked. Was Gloria serious or poking fun at her? "Can you at least turn around so I can put my jeans back on?" She didn't want to face off with a murder suspect in her panties. And nothing put her more at a disadvantage than feeling a breeze on her backside.

Gloria didn't move. She probably felt like she had the upper hand. "What do you know about the NASA security breach?"

Raina considered lying, but she had already told Gloria she had information about the breach previously. So no bimbolina card here. But she couldn't very well tell Gloria everything.

Though Matthew had evidence that Claire brokered the sale, Raina had no proof of Gloria's role. The two women could have been in cahoots previously but had a falling out in this recent breach.

"I overheard you accusing Claire Boucher of

stealing research from your computer. And now Claire is dead," Raina said.

Gloria studied Raina for a long moment. "What are you implying?"

"I don't know. You tell me. Where were you at the time of Claire's death?"

"I was upstairs in my room, getting ready for the morning."

"So you have no alibi?"

"I have no reason for killing Claire."

"Once the breach is discovered, isn't your security clearance in jeopardy? This is a pretty strong motive."

Gloria clenched her jaw. Her lips pressed into a thin line as if to stop herself from giving too much away.

Raina thought about the morning she'd tried to get Po Po a spot at the convention. When she handed her contact information to Claire, there was a cell phone on the table. By the time Brian placed both hands on the table to face off with Claire, the cell phone was gone.

"And you stole Claire's cell phone. You probably hacked her passcode and got into her messages and emails," Raina said. "Even if you wiped for prints and discarded the phone, the forensic team would still be able to use the cell towers to pinpoint where it traveled." Actually, she didn't think the technology was sophisticated enough for this, but it sounded plausible.

"Stealing someone's cell phone is a petty crime. It's not the same as murder," Gloria said.

"You're right. Stealing a phone does not necessarily mean you killed Claire. However, from the emails or messages, you probably found out about her appointment in the laundry room. Not only do you have a motive and no alibi, but now you have an opportunity to kill her. Sounds like an open and shut case." It wasn't, but Raina was counting on Gloria's lack of experience with the court system to get her to start talking.

Gloria was quiet for a long moment as if considering the full implication of what Raina just said. "What's your role in this? Why do you care?"

"My fiancé was hired by NASA to deal with the security breaches. If you're innocent, he can help you."

Gloria rose from the sofa. Indecision flickered across her face. The last of her bravado disappeared, and her lower lip trembled like she was trying to hold back tears. She looked as if she finally figured out that she was in over her head and didn't know how to get out of the situation.

Raina threw off the bed covers, ignoring her half-dressed stage. If Gloria decided to flee, Raina was running after her. She had waited too long to get answers from this woman to let her slip away. It wasn't as if Hendricks and his staff hadn't had a full view of her tighty whities before.

They held each other's gaze for a long moment. They were so focused on each other, Raina barely heard the door click open. Movement from the corner of her eye caught her attention. She shifted her gaze to find Little Richie walking into her suite.

Raina's jaw dropped. The man was an impersonator with greasepaint on his face and a wig on his head. The backs of his hands were blotchy like the impersonator was too impatient with the makeup work. He was tall and well-muscled, reminding Raina of her fiancé. What was the point of a lock when anyone could waltz in and out of her room like there was a revolving door?

Gloria's head swiveled to the door and froze.

Little Richie came in, closing the door behind him. Though he wasn't holding a weapon, the air thickened with a sense of danger.

Raina's gaze scanned the room, looking for a weapon. She didn't know who this person was or why he was in her room, but a surge of adrenaline ran down her spine. What if Claire Boucher didn't work alone, and he was one of her cohorts? Or the Russian spy who normally bought the stolen information?

Little Richie glanced at Raina and held her gaze. The familiar gold-flecked brown eyes knocked the wind out of her. Matthew? Had her fiancé been the Little Richie impersonator all along? She had run into this person multiple times over the last several days. And wasn't he at the police station at the moment?

Gloria dashed for the door, but Matthew stepped in front of her. She backed up until her knees hit the coffee table.

"I'm Matthew Louie, and I work for the Inspector

General's Office," Matthew said, whipping out a badge from his back pocket. "I'm here to escort you to the FBI building for questioning."

"What does the FBI want with me?" Gloria asked, her voice trembling.

"It's NASA who wants to talk with you. The FBI building is the nearest secure federal facility," Matthew said.

Gloria lunged for Raina with the lipstick stun gun, and Matthew hurled himself toward the bed. But Gloria pivoted on her heels and grabbed the door. She flung it open to find Hendricks and several other men waiting for her in the hall. The fight went out of Gloria when she realized there weren't enough prayers in the world to get through this many men.

Matthew got up and went to the door. "Give me two minutes." He shut the door and joined Raina on the bed. He swept her up in a bear hug. "Are you okay?" he mumbled into her hair.

Raina tried to nod but couldn't move her head. "Yes, but you're cutting off my oxygen supply." She was still trying to process what happened.

Matthew released her. "I don't have time to explain, but I knew she would come for you eventually."

"Who? Gloria?"

He nodded. "I was by the exit next to the stage in the main hall when you mentioned the NASA breach to her. I couldn't believe you would put yourself in the line of fire like that, but once I got over the anger, I decided to stick close by and wait."

"If you knew Gloria would seek me out, then why did you have Detective Stafford"—Raina made air quotes with her fingers—"arrest you by the pool?"

"So Gloria would know I'm miles away from the hotel-casino. She wouldn't have shown up otherwise. I think she was on to me from the moment I made the arrangements to buy the information from Claire."

"So they were in it together? I really thought Gloria was the victim."

"I did at first too, but when you told me Gloria confronted Claire publicly, I knew it was a ruse. She would have been in the clear if she had stayed home in California. Instead, she came here supposedly to confront Claire and then promptly meet up with a known Russian spy."

Raina frowned. "Who was the spy?"

"When you spoke to her, he was there in the alcove. Luckily, he was spooked by your presence and decided it wasn't worth hanging around to recover the USB stick."

"I thought I was interrupting a lovers' tryst. Gloria must be upset I've blown the deal. And so she came after me."

Matthew nodded. "You're one lucky woman, Rainy."

"Do you think Gloria would have harmed me?"

Matthew hesitated. "I don't know. Gloria is an opportunist. Selling a secret or two would have given her enough money to retire to a beach in Mexico. But

with everything falling apart, and no job to return to..."
He shrugged. "Your guess is as good as any."

Raina shivered.

Matthew gave her a reassuring wink. "I'm sure you would have been able to take care of yourself." He gestured at his bruised nose and blackened eye. "Look at how you took care of me."

Raina smiled and kissed him gently.

"I have to go with her, but I promise to come back as soon as I can." Matthew kissed Raina again and left.

After the chaos moments before, the room was eerily silent. Raina glanced around uneasily and slipped on her jeans. She studied the untampered lock on the door. Maybe she should ask the front desk for a different room.

She had seen the Little Richie impersonator several times in the last few days. At the time, she hadn't thought much about it, but now she realized it had been the perfect disguise for her fiancé. Everyone had been too busy trying to get a selfie with him rather than to question his movements.

Raina gathered the contents of her wallet and returned them to their slots, noting that Gloria had stolen all her cash and a credit card. She dialed her credit card company and put it on the speaker mode.

While the computer prompts verified her identity and information, Raina returned to packing her purse. She tossed away the old receipts and an ancient cough drop. The computer voice announced that they appreciate her business but the wait time was ten minutes.

She sighed. At least she didn't have to worry about Gloria maxing out her credit card during the wait.

A representative came on the line at the same time Maggie's call flashed on the screen. Raina dismissed Maggie's call. She didn't want to go through the whole song and dance again with the credit card company and start over on the queue.

While in the middle of her conversation with an Indian man who said his name was David, her cell phone chirped to indicate she got a voicemail. She frowned. If Maggie left a message, maybe her call was important after all. She finished up her conversation with the credit card company and dialed her voicemail.

Maggie's panicked voice came on.

"Rainy, your grandma is missing. Call me back."

19

———

M.I.A.

Raina called her grandma, but it went straight to voicemail. She tried Maggie next and got the same result. Frank picked up on the first ring.

"What happened?" Raina asked.

"Your grandma got ahead of us going into the exhibit hall," Frank said. "By the time Maggie and I got to the stage up front, she was gone. We screamed her name and looked everywhere, but we couldn't find her."

"What was she looking for?"

"The gift baskets."

"Why?"

"Your grandma mentioned something about things not adding up."

"Where are you now?" Raina heard music in the background.

"We're standing outside the main hall. I got on

stage and asked if anyone had seen your grandma. We told the audience we would stand by the door if they have information for us."

"How long have you been waiting?"

"About five minutes."

"That's too soon for you to leave. While you hang out there, I will check with the security team. Maybe Po Po will show up on one of the video surveillance feeds."

Raina tossed the rest of her stuff back into her purse and ran out of the room. She didn't bother to check the door lock on her way out like she normally did. Either it latched closed, or it didn't.

When she knocked on the door of security headquarters, it didn't open. She knocked again. She dialed Hendricks's cell phone, and it went to voicemail. She knocked again. Finally, the pregnant woman cracked open the door.

"Yes?" the pregnant security guard said.

"Is Hendricks here? I need help locating my grandma," Raina said. She took a deep breath. Her voice held a tinge of panic. It would not help her grandma if people didn't understand her.

"The boss is escorting the terrorist to the FBI building."

Raina blinked. When did Gloria get elevated to the role of a terrorist? "Can you track down my grandma on the video feeds?"

"How long has your grandma been missing?"

Raina glanced at the time stamp of Maggie's

message on her phone. Had her grandma only been missing for thirty minutes? "Half an hour ago."

"Did you try calling her?"

"Yes. Can you look through your video feeds?"

"No, ma'am. I'm not authorized to do this. It's to protect the privacy of our guests."

"I'm sure if Hendricks were here, he would allow this."

"But he's not here," the pregnant security guard said matter-of-factly.

"Can you call him?"

"No, ma'am. Then it'll look like I can't handle things when he's not around. We're working on improving my leadership skills."

Raina took another deep breath. Ramming her head against the wall would be less painful than this. "How else might I get to see video footage?"

"I am authorized to show them when there's a warrant."

No judge would give Raina a warrant. "What if Willie gives me permission to see the video footage?"

The pregnant security guard shrugged. "She's the big boss. I must do what she wants." She went back inside the command center and shut the door.

Raina balled her hands into fists and let out a scream in frustration. She spun on her heels and ran to the elevator. Willie wasn't inside her office. Neither was she in any of the administrative offices.

Back at the elevator foyer, she called Frank again.

"I can't find anyone in the hotel to help me. Any luck down there?" Raina asked.

"No."

"I'm going back to the rooms. Maybe Po Po went back to charge her phone."

Raina hung up and glanced at the battery bar on her phone. There was less than five percent of juice left. She had plugged it in before napping, but Gloria must have unplugged it. Maybe she should change her passwords, especially to the apps that were constantly logged in like her email. Maybe later.

She bounced impatiently on the balls of her feet while the elevator made its slow progress to the eighth floor. Her grandma had declared they were staying at the luckiest floor in the hotel-casino when they checked in. Eight was the homonym for wealth in Chinese. But to Raina, it felt like their luck was running backwards the longer they stayed here.

Raina flung open the door to Maggie's suite using the spare keycard in her purse. "Po Po, are you in here?"

No response.

She strolled into the bedroom and even opened the closet. Nope. She checked the bathroom. Nope. She went back to the bedroom and checked under each of the queen-size beds. Nope.

She dialed her grandma's cell phone again. It went to voicemail.

"Po Po, it's Rainy. We're getting concerned about your safety. Please call us back."

Raina texted the same message. When she checked the battery bar, it was now at three percent. Her cell phone would be as useful as a brick in a few minutes. She returned to her room and plugged in her cell phone to charge it. She did the same routine, checking the bathroom, the closet, and underneath the king-size bed. No dice.

Po Po had only been gone for about forty-five minutes. Maybe she was in a bathroom somewhere with a diarrhea attack. There was no need to worry. This was probably a silly misunderstanding where the senior citizens got confused about the meeting location.

And yet, Po Po was a big stickler for synchronizing their watches and checking in when they were in the middle of an operation. The suspects would have no reason to kidnap her grandma because they didn't know about Raina and Po Po's relationship. Raina had questioned each of them on her own.

Nooo, wait. When she had questioned Brian Anderson, her grandma was with her and then she went into the laundry room to inquire about their costumes. Raina frowned, trying to picture Brian as the killer maid.

He was slight enough at about five foot six inches, maybe a hundred and forty pounds. He would have no problem fitting into a maid's T-shirt. Plastic glasses were easy enough to find. If he popped out the lenses, even reading glasses or sunglasses would do in a pinch. And half the people walking around the building had on a wig. Was it possible that Po Po found evidence linking Brian to the murder and confronted him?

Raina glanced at the door, waiting for a sign on what to do next. Her gaze traveled from the lock to the carpet. She squinted. There was a slip of paper from underneath the door. It was too early for the invoice of their stay because they weren't supposed to check out for another day. Her heart rate picked up a tempo, banging against her chest.

"Please don't let this be a ransom note," she whispered.

When she picked up the folded sheet of paper, her hand trembled. It was plain white, and she could see printed words on the other side. She opened the paper. Taped to the corner was a lock of silvery white hair with red streaks in it.

Loading dock. 6 pm. Tell no one.

Raina's heart stopped for a moment and resumed its beating. Was Brian still outside in the hall? She grabbed the lipstick stun gun and jerked open the door. There was no one in the hallway. She ran down to the elevator but didn't see anyone either. She jogged back to her room to study the message again.

She couldn't tell Frank and Maggie about the letter. The two senior citizens would want to set up an ambush or something that might jeopardize her grandma's safety. If only Raina could borrow Poe. With his previous owner, the service dog was once a ferocious guard dog.

Raina tapped the screen on her cell phone. It was already five forty-five, and there was only one percent battery life left. Her phone wasn't charging, but she didn't have time to fiddle with it.

She dialed Detective Stafford's number, and it went straight to voicemail. He might be with Matthew at the FBI building. She left him a message about her missing grandma and the contents of the note. Next, she dialed Matthew's phone number. She left him the same message.

"I'm going downstairs to find my grandmother. I love you," Raina said.

Before she could hang up the call, the screen went dark and powered off. She stared at the useless device in her hand. Maybe she could chuck it at Brian's head.

Fear settled like a concrete block on her chest, and she had a difficult time breathing. The rendezvous at the loading dock was a trap, but she had to go anyway. There wasn't enough time to do anything but show up with her bravado and pray the cavalry would arrive on time. Even if Matthew or Detective Stafford heard the message and left immediately, it would still take forty minutes to an hour to get here with the traffic. She was very much on her own.

Raina took a deep breath and closed her eyes. She prayed for her ancestors to look out for her grandma. Whatever might happen, she was not alone. There were several generations of goodwill and blessing to protect her from evil. If she stayed calm and used her wits, she would walk away from this confrontation. She had to believe this.

Her gaze swept the room, looking for weapons. She had her lipstick stun gun and pepper spray. Those went into the pockets of her capris. The hotel pen could be jammed into an eye or the throat in a grapple. She twisted her hair into a knot and stuck the pen in the nest to hold it in place. With her eager armor, she slipped out of the room to rescue her grandma.

20

LADY WITH A SWORD

Raina tapped on the call button for the elevator. She had about six minutes to get down to the loading dock. Brian probably expected her to go through the service hall and out to the side exit. This was the most direct route from inside the hotel-casino. But if Raina went through the casino floor and around from the outside, she might have a chance at surprising him.

She stepped into the elevator and hit the button for the first floor. As the car descended, she thought through all the possibilities. What if she approached the loading dock through the hedges? There might be enough shadows to hide her approach.

Raina tucked her chin and power walked through the casino, avoiding all eye contact. No one called out to her, which meant Maggie and Frank were still waiting by the exhibit hall. Thank goodness. As much as she would like backup, the two senior citizens weren't it.

When she stepped out of the hotel-casino, the sky was a fading smoky purple with the sun setting behind a skyscraper. The laundry was done for the day, so the storage and laundry rooms were locked up. And Brian couldn't tie up and carry her grandma to the loading dock through the hotel-casino without drawing unwanted attention. And Po Po wasn't someone who would follow him meekly, so he must have knocked her out. The thought made Raina's blood boil.

As she rounded the corner of the building, she ducked and crabwalked across the footpath and into the hedges. Once within the shadows, she straightened, thankful for the cover from the towering holly oak trees. By coming out from the front of the building, her eyes had already adjusted to the reduced light. Brian Anderson leaned against the wall next to the side door, smoking a cigarette. There was no sign of her grandma anywhere.

Brian was dressed in skinny black jeans and a black maid shirt. He wore some kind of padding underneath the shirt, so it looked as if his chest were an A cup. He had on a honey blonde wig that fell to his shoulders. In the dim lighting and from far away, he looked like a woman.

Raina's gaze traveled to the open guitar case on the ground in front of him. There were handcuffs, a whip, and a samurai sword. Maybe he was planning to go to a Fifty Shades party afterward. She shuddered at the thought. Obviously, he no longer felt the need to hide or explain why he murdered Claire Boucher. And from his casual posture and nonchalant air, he seemed to believe that he had the upper hand in this situation.

Unless her grandma was strapped to an explosive, and he held the trigger device, Raina didn't have to confront him. She doubted that he had the expertise or the equipment to assemble a bomb on such short notice. The murder and the kidnapping were the actions of a two-bit opportunist pushed to his limit, not a criminal mastermind.

A mosquito landed on Raina's neck, and she flapped her hand to get rid of it. A trickle of sweat ran down the small of her back. She could wait for Brian to leave and then follow him because he would probably check on her grandma to make sure she wasn't rescued while he was here. But she probably didn't have the stealth to sneak around behind him.

"Come out, come out, little mouse," Brian called out, flicking his cigarette onto the ground.

Raina's heart raced, and her shoulders ached with tension. How did he know she was here? Maybe he was just bluffing. If she stayed where she was and kept quiet...

"I know you're out there, Raina Sun," Brian said. He bent down and picked up the whip and strapped on the samurai sword to his waist. "If you don't come out, then I'll have to use these toys on your granny."

Something popped like a bubble inside of Raina,

and the fear disappeared to be replaced by a boiling hot anger. How dare he threaten to harm her grandma.

"She's inside the trash bin. Come out before she runs out of oxygen," Brian said.

Raina's gaze shifted to the concrete wall surrounding the trash bins. From her vantage point, she couldn't see the metal containers, so she had no way of verifying what he said without giving away her position.

Her gaze shifted to the window panel on the side door. Even with binoculars, she would have been looking at the storage room. If she came out to inspect the underbrush of the holly oak grove a few days ago, she would have known he lied about being Claire's lookout. This was a costly lesson that Raina hoped her grandma didn't have to pay for with her life.

"Why did you kill Claire? For ten thousand dollars?" Raina called out.

Brian's head snapped up, and he squinted at the shadows of the holly oak trees. He hesitated for a moment as if debating whether to hack through the hedges and drag her out. "She wanted to ask the board to do an audit going back the last five years."

Raina did some quick math. If he had embezzled ten thousand dollars a year, that was equal to fifty thousand dollars in the last five years. Somehow she knew in her gut that he had been doing this for far longer than five years.

"You have been skimming off the top for that long,

huh? How did you find out about Claire's appointment in the laundry room?" Raina asked.

"I stole her cell phone. The passcode was easy enough. It was her husband's birthday."

Raina's eyes widened. She really thought that Gloria had stolen the phone.

"Imagine my surprise to find that Miss Goody Two Shoes is selling top-secret research to the Russians," Brian continued. "I should be given a medal for doing my part to help our country. I'm a hero."

The man was clearly delusional. Raina sidestepped to the left, getting closer to the concrete wall. Her gaze traveled the width of the wall. There were no footholds to scale it. And even if she could climb it, what would she do next? Dance on the lid of the trash bin while he slashed at her feet?

There was a gap of about four feet where if she dashed for the wall, he could pounce on her with either the whip or the sword. She didn't have protection against either weapon. What she needed was a distraction where she could get close enough to use either the stun gun or the pepper spray. She pulled both items from her pocket and moved the trigger to the "on" position for the pepper spray.

Several moments passed in silence. Raina's neck ached from the tension, and her fingers were cramping from hovering over the triggers for both her meager weapons. At this rate, they both could stand here for hours. Her body was trembling from the after-effects of the initial adrenaline rush. If she didn't do something soon, her moment of bravery might disappear, and she might curl up into a ball.

Maybe Brian was feeling the same way about the impasse. He strolled closer to the trash bins. "If you don't come out, I'll stab into the trash bins. Bleeding to death is a painful way to die." He banged open the lid.

Raina took a deep breath and strolled out from the safety of the hedges. "So are you planning to hack me to death? Someone is bound to hear my screams."

Brian returned to the guitar case, grabbed the handcuffs, and threw them toward Raina. "Put them on. We're going for a ride." He snapped the whip. The crack sounded like a mini-explosion in the stillness.

Raina flinched. He looked like he knew how to use the thing. Her armpits suddenly went damp. Her thin shirt would shred to ribbons in a matter of minutes from the whip. "My grandma isn't in the trash bin, is she? You have her stashed in a vehicle."

Her voice trembled, and Raina hated how weak she sounded. He was probably planning to drive them out into the desert to dispose of them. They were less than five feet apart. It wouldn't take much effort for Brian to step forward and snap the whip like a lion trainer at Raina's face. A mosquito landed on the back of her neck again, but she didn't dare move a muscle. She was afraid to spook him with a sudden movement.

Brian's eyes shifted from Raina's face to an area above her shoulder. He frowned as if noticing something. "You're too smart for your own good. Now put the cuffs on."

Raina blinked, straining her ears. What was the noise? Sounded like something jingling. Keys? Was someone coming?

"...I saw her go this way..."

"...take off the leash..."

A sense of hope filled Raina. Someone was coming. If she kept Brian talking, someone could get close enough to see a strange woman wielding a whip and a samurai sword.

Brian must have heard the sound too. "Put the cuffs on," he hissed.

Raina kept her eyes on Brian's face and bent to retrieve the handcuffs. A low rumbling growl seemed to come out of nowhere. The fine hair on the back of her neck stiffened. She froze in her crouched position.

Movement from the corner of her eye caught Raina's attention. A dark streak moved at a breakneck speed. Brian's expression changed from uncertainty to horror. A large black Labrador retriever flew at Brian, his sharp white teeth clamping onto the arm holding the whip. Poe!

Brian screamed and beat at the service dog. They jerked about the small footpath like drunken dance partners. The dog continued to growl. Beads of blood scattered around them onto the concrete floor.

Raina straightened, powering on the stun gun. Brian stumbled and he shifted. When Raina saw Brian's exposed back, she ran up and hit him with the stun gun. His body stiffened and arched. She held on as Brian dropped to one knee.

"Off, Poe! Off," Maggie called out from behind them.

The service dog shook his head one more time before removing his teeth from Brian's arm. He growled and backed away from Brian. His body was alert and ready to pounce again.

Frank came up and handcuffed Brian. The villain lay on the concrete, panting.

"Search his pockets for car keys," Raina said.

Frank rolled Brian over until he lay on his back and patted his pockets. He pulled out a set of keys and held it out. "Found them."

Raina grabbed the keys. "Call the police. Check the trash bins. He said Po Po was in the trash a moment ago. I'm checking the parking lot for his car. She might be in his trunk."

Raina moved toward the parking lot around the building. As she moved from car to car, she pressed the remote, listening for the chirp. After the first row, she grew worried. Wouldn't Brian try to get a parking spot closer to the loading dock? In the second row, toward the end, a black SUV's headlight flashed and chirped.

She ran toward the SUV and peered in through the driver's window. There was no one in the backseat. She unlocked the trunk. It popped up on her face, and she staggered backward, clutching at her nose. Blood squirted out from between her fingers. The middle of her forehead throbbed. Now she knew how her fiancé felt when she had clobbered him.

The trunk lid opened. Po Po screamed muffled

curses, swung her bound hands, and kicked her tied up legs. When she saw the blood on Raina's face, she grew quiet and stopped her jerking motions. At least Raina could tell people her grandma wasn't going down without a fight.

21

WEDDING MARCH

The next morning Raina woke up with a song in her heart and wings on her feet. She was getting married today. Unfortunately, she was also sharing the bathroom with another bride. Her grandma had insisted the men sleep in Raina's suite, so the women ended up in one suite. Something about it being unlucky for the grooms to see the brides before the wedding. The plan was for the women to spend most of the day at the spa for a massage, hair, and makeup. Then they were to rendezvous with the men at the chapel downstairs at their appointed time.

The makeup lady was obviously distressed, powdering and repowdering Raina's nose. She looked Raina in the eye and said, "Honey, if he's already beating you like this, think about what he'll do after he buys the cow. It ain't worth it."

Raina blinked. The false lashes felt weird on her eyes.

"It wasn't my grandson who beat her black and blue. It was her grandma," Maggie said, jerking her thumb at her best friend.

Po Po blushed, heat rising from her neck to inflame her face. "How was I supposed to know she was rescuing me?"

Raina burst out laughing until tears ran down her face, smearing the makeup. And then all four of them were laughing, undoing much of the makeup lady's work.

Later, they returned to the suite to get dressed. Maggie put on a midnight blue satin dress with a beaded top. Her wispy white hair was brushed out. The hairdresser clipped a crystal orchid on the side of her head, adding a touch of whimsical to the outfit. Her second grandma looked beautiful.

After helping Maggie dress, Raina reached into her suitcase for her serviceable lavender dress. She had paid quite a bit of money for it a few years ago, and she had only worn it once.

Before she could slip it on, Po Po cried out, "Not that old thing, my dear girl. We got you something better."

Maggie went into the closet and pulled out a garment bag. Both grandmas smiled at Raina, their eyes twinkling. They probably spent the last two days picking out the perfect dress for her special day.

Raina's heart sank. Knowing her grandma's taste, she was afraid to look in the bag. She didn't want to walk down the aisle in a dress that bound her like a sausage and popped her girls out on top. There might be even a ventilation flap or two on the sides and in the rear to round it all up.

She couldn't say no. If it weren't for the grandmas, she probably wouldn't end up getting married at all. They had booked a double wedding, which said they either had a lot of hope or faith. But she really didn't want to look like a girl in a rock video.

Raina took a deep breath and unzipped the garment bag. Her eyes widened at the simple sleeveless chiffon dress. She could feel the burning behind her eyes, and she blinked rapidly, hoping to keep the tears from wrecking her makeup again.

Po Po beamed at Maggie. "I think she likes it."

When the trio headed downstairs in their wedding finery, people stopped and stared. Among the rock star impersonators and tourists with their huge cameras, they were like peacocks among the pigeons.

Outside the chapel, Po Po made Maggie and Raina wait while she went in to check things out. Her grandma was taking her role as bridesmaid seriously. Either that or she felt guilty for giving Raina a goose egg on her forehead and a swollen nose. Luckily, she didn't end up with a black eye.

"Okay, it's showtime," Po Po said, popping out from the chapel. She held the door open for them.

They went in and stood at the small foyer area. The "Wedding March" played from the speakers installed around the chapel. Raina's gaze made a beeline for the wedding arch at the front of the chapel.

Matthew stood to one side in his black tuxedo with his hands clasped behind him, his feet slightly spread. With a bruised nose and a black eye, he looked more like a pirate captain than a groom. When their eyes met, his expression didn't change, though it seemed as if his face lit up from within. Raina felt a goofy smile spreading across her face. Her fiancé could pretend to be stoic, but she knew from the twinkle in his eyes that he was smiling right back at her.

Po Po went down the aisle first. Then it was Maggie's turn. When it was Raina's turn, she looked straight ahead and hoped she wouldn't trip on her heels. From the corner of her eye, she saw a handful of people sitting in the pews. She didn't know if they were paid witnesses, wedding crashers, or tourists resting their feet away from the crowd.

Her gaze never left Matthew's eyes. When Raina reached his side, he reached out to clasp her hands. A tremor ran up her arm. When she realized the shaking came from him, her grin widened. So the stoic face hid his nerves.

The wedding officiant started the ceremony. Raina wondered if Matthew was considering fleeing at the moment. This would be his last chance. With his grandma in attendance, this marriage wouldn't get annulled like last time. This marriage would be forever.

Raina scanned Matthew's eyes. He tightened his grip on her hands, and his shaking stopped. There wasn't a hint of a shadow in his gold-flecked brown eyes. They held a depth of love that stole her breath away.

After Maggie and Frank repeated the lines that pledged them to each other, Raina and Matthew did the same.

"And now, you may kiss the brides," the wedding officiant said.

Raina closed her eyes and rose to her tippy toes. Matthew leaned down and kissed her. A soft feather kiss that was full of promises. His sage and clean water scent filled her head with thoughts of the future.

The men congratulated and shook each other's hands. At one point, Matthew was pumping two hands at the same time. Po Po spoke and hugged Maggie too.

Raina's gaze shifted to the back of the chapel. She locked eyes with a Chinese man in his late fifties. He was in a white linen suit with salt and pepper hair. He raised a champagne glass as if to toast the wedding couples.

She frowned. The man looked familiar. Where had she seen him before?

"Congratulations," the man mouthed. And the years melted away. The twinkling gold-flecked brown eyes were a mirror image of Matthew's eyes. The man was his father.

Raina's smile wavered, and she nodded in acknowledgement of his well wishes. So Matthew's father showed up after all to attend his mother and his son's wedding.

The man put a finger to his lips. He didn't want his family to know he was here.

Raina hesitated. Maggie would welcome her son with joy and tears, but Matthew might have the opposite reaction. Did Raina want to ruin Matthew's memory of their wedding day? And if she kept quiet, would he be upset about it later? And why didn't her father-in-law want his family to know he was here?

Matthew touched her arm and drew her closer by his side. She broke eye contact to look up at her fiancé's smiling face. Frank said something that made Matthew burst out laughing. It was a rare sight to see her husband this relaxed and happy. But she shouldn't keep his father's presence from Matthew. This could be the start of a reconciliation.

"Matthew, honey," Raina whispered into his ear.

He glanced down at her. Maybe she looked anxious because he was instantly alert, flipping on cop mode in the blink of an eye.

She pointed at the rear of the chapel to an empty pew.

Matthew's gaze followed the direction of her finger. "What is it?"

Raina frowned. "There was a man in the corner. He toasted us with a champagne glass, but he's not there anymore."

"He must be a tourist who wants to see a Las Vegas wedding." Matthew kissed the goose egg on her forehead. "I can't believe we look like this on our wedding day."

Raina cupped his face in her hands. "At least we're evenly matched." And she kissed him.

THE END

Chilly Comforts and Disasters
(Raina Sun #9)
Available now!

ACKNOWLEDGMENTS

A story is a dream that a writer brings to life on paper. But a book needs a team to nurture it into an enjoyable experience.

I want to thank my editors, Alicia S. and Brandee, for wrangling my words so they are coherent.

And then, there are my beta-readers—Marion D., Debi P., Joyce S., Susan J., and Sharon S.—thank you, ladies, for volunteering your time to catch these sneaky typos and grammatical errors.

Also, thanks to service dog, Poe, for lending your name to Maggie Louie's service dog in the story.

And finally, thank you, Susan C. for the awesome cover.

I wouldn't have been able to bring this story to life
without all of you.

—Anne R. Tan

Fair Cronies and Felonies (Raina Sun Mystery #10)

How about another series by Anne R. Tan?

Just Shoot Me Dead (Lucy Fong #1)

Just Lost and Found (Lucy Fong #1.5)

Just a Lucy Break-In (Lucy Fong #2)

CHILLY COMFORTS AND DISASTERS

"I need to ask you for a favor," Blue said, turning the disposable coffee cup around and around in his hand. His voice was smooth with a trace of a European accent.

Raina and her brother-in-law stood around the kitchen island. It was the only place downstairs that was relatively free of debris and other construction material.

The avocado green appliances were still functional but were energy hogs. The tangerine-colored walls were an easy fix. Luckily, they were on schedule, which meant she could have a decent kitchen within the next two months.

Her grandma had brought over an electric kettle and boxes of instant coffee and tea on the first day of construction. This thoughtful gesture had saved more than one strained nerve in the last eleven months of her house remodel nightmare.

Sebastian "Blue" Luc's mother was Italian, so he inherited the hazel eyes and olive skin tone. From his Chinese father, he got the black hair and the gold flecks in his eyes.

Blue was more muscular and solid than his brother, which suited his profession as a general contractor, while Matthew was lean and wiry with a runner's physique. They were different enough outwardly that it took Raina a while to figure out the two of them were related.

Raina hesitated. She felt like a jerk for not saying yes right away, but whenever a family member asked for a favor—no matter how small—it always turned out to be complicated. And in this case, it would impact both sides of the family if there were hurt feelings. Not only was Blue her brother-in-law, but he was also married to Raina's cousin. One side or both sides of the family would undoubtedly complain about Raina's involvement at the end.

Blue had not only given them a great deal on the remodel work, but he also came through with finding them significant discounts. She sighed inwardly. Familial obligation and human decency meant she had to help.

"Let me guess. Does this have anything to do with your dad?" Raina asked.

Blue's eyes widened. "How did you know? Did he get in touch with you about getting together for Thanksgiving dinner?"

Wayne Louie had appeared briefly in Raina's Las

Vegas wedding several months ago. Matthew didn't see him in the crowd. Since then, she had been walking around with this secret, waiting for the other shoe to drop.

"Is he inviting us to dinner? Or does he want to show up for dinner?" Raina asked, hoping it would buy her a few precious seconds on how to react.

Matthew wouldn't want anything to do with his estranged father. Wayne was an alcoholic who turned abusive when drunk. His apologies afterward weren't worth much. He had left when Matthew was still in elementary school. And one day, his mother showed up at Ah Ma's doorstep to drop Matthew off and never came back.

At the time, Raina was too young to understand the full implication of these events, but now she understood what was never spoken. While the scars had scabbed over enough for the man to function, her husband was not a whole man.

Blue shrugged and gave her a sheepish look. "Since Dad is coming from out of town, he's inviting himself over for Thanksgiving."

Raina grimaced inwardly. She had the option of either inviting her father-in-law to join her extended family for dinner in San Francisco or hosting it in her newly remodeled house. She did some mental arithmetic. If they were lucky, the house would be completed at the end of October, giving her just a few weeks to move in and get ready for Thanksgiving.

The timing was tight. It would be insanely stressful

up until feast day. And Matthew would not thank her for interfering. But even if a reconciliation wasn't possible, confronting his dad might help Matthew bury his demons. It might make him whole.

"What does Ah Ma think about this?" Raina asked.

"She said it's up to Matthew."

In other words, Maggie Louie didn't want to have to pick between her son and grandson. And Raina didn't blame her one bit. She should take her cue from her grandma-in-law.

"Let me think about it," Raina said.

"Is this a 'yes, let me think about it' or a 'no, let me think about it'?" Blue asked.

Raina ignored his question. She didn't know which answer would correctly describe how she felt. "We both know how Matthew feels about this. I don't see him agreeing to it."

"We don't have to tell Matthew about it until the day before. If you give him a warning, he will call the whole thing off."

Raina shook her head. Her loyalty lay with her husband. "I'm not walking around with this secret for the next few weeks." Wayne's presence at her wedding didn't count. By the time she had pointed out the corner of the chapel to Matthew, her father-in-law had left.

"It's—"

Bam!

The wall between the kitchen and living room shook. Dust floated in the air.

Raina's eyes widened, and she grabbed hold of the kitchen island. What was that? An earthquake? But the ground felt steady enough underneath her feet.

Blue set his mug on the kitchen island. "If those numbskulls started tearing down the wall..." He picked up his hard hat and strode toward the entryway to the hall.

Bam! Bam!

Raina jumped at the noise and ran after him. A sudden spike in adrenaline caused her heart to beat more rapidly. So no earthquake, but a laborer who didn't know how to follow directions. Yikes! Depending on the damage, this might blow their already tight budget.

Blue skidded to a stop at the entryway to the living room. Technically, the room was probably called a parlor more than a hundred years ago. His mouth opened and closed twice without uttering a sound.

Raina followed his lead and stopped at the entryway. She peered in, and her jaw dropped.

The head of a sledgehammer was wedged into the drywall. Po Po held onto the handle with both hands and a foot braced against the wall, pulling at it with all her strength. Instead of safety glasses, she had on swimming goggles. A fine coat of white dust covered her entire face and much of her upper torso.

Her grandma wore a pink hard hat with skulls and crossbones stickers all around it, a neon green safety vest, and black steel toe boots. Underneath the safety gear was a neon orange T-shirt and leggings. Her silver hair had streaks of pink in it. Even from a mile away, a person would have to be blind to miss her grandma.

In contrast, Raina wore a worn T-shirt and baggy jeans. She had on safety boots—left behind from her previous career as an engineer—an old hard hat that probably no longer met the standards, and safety glasses. Her curly black hair was tucked in a messy ponytail.

When Po Po caught sight of them, she let go of the handle and placed the swimming goggles on her forehead. It looked like two pairs of eyes were peering at them. She jerked a thumb at the grapefruit-size hole in the wall. "I got started for you. Feel free to take over anytime."

Blue gaped at her. Newly married into the family, he still tiptoed around the matriarch of the family. Unlike Raina, who found her grandma's antics hilarious, he didn't know when she was joking or if the matriarch of the family might be going senile as the rumor had it. He raised an eyebrow at Raina as if to say it was her circus.

Raina sighed inwardly. Most days, she found her grandma's antics hilarious, but today was not one of them. "Po Po, what are you doing? You can't just start demoing the walls without, ah, professional guidance." She didn't want to get her grandma's tail up in the air. Like a cat, sometimes, her grandma's ego had to be properly managed.

"The two of you just kept yapping in the kitchen.

Somebody's got to start the work. Rainy, you can't finish in time if you don't put in the sweat equity," Po Po said. She gave the sledgehammer another tug and handed it to Raina. "Imagine the loan officer's face. Now take your frustration out on the wall." She stepped back to join Blue at the entryway.

Blue gave the senior citizen a sideways glance and took a side step, creating more distance between them. Yep, he was firmly in the senile camp. It was a good thing Matthew didn't share his half-brother's view on the subject.

Raina tested the weight of the sledgehammer in her hand. It was about twenty pounds. Heavy enough to do some serious damage, but not so much that she could hurt herself. She swung the sledgehammer, and it connected with the drywall. Dust flew out, and she turned her head, blinking and coughing.

When she finally could speak again, she said, "I thought this was supposed to be fun. The people on *Fixer Upper* always seemed to be enjoying themselves."

Po Po wiggled her fingers. "It's called TV magic. Do you think reality TV is actually real? It's still scripted." She bounced on her toes and stretched out her hands. "My turn again. My turn. I got plenty of people I would like to take a swing at." She stepped into the room and reached for the sledgehammer.

Blue's eyes widened. He stepped forward and lifted the sledgehammer off of Po Po's hands. "Whoa, stallion. We wouldn't want you to pull a muscle."

Raina groaned inwardly. This was exactly the wrong thing to say to her grandma. His tone was teasing but also slightly patronizing. While it could be fun to watch Po Po eat him for breakfast, Raina needed Blue to finish the house remodel.

Po Po straightened and placed her hands on her hips. "What did you say?"

Raina linked arms with her grandma and tugged her back a step. "Why don't we let Blue finish the job? It's not as fun as it looks on TV. The sledgehammer is heavy. I was worried about dropping it on my toes the entire time."

Po Po harrumphed and gave Raina a sideways glance as if she knew what Raina was thinking. "Only for you, Rainy. Anyone else, and I would kick in his teeth." She spoke with a fake Brooklyn accent.

Even though Po Po grew up in a wealthy merchant family in China and learned English from the missionaries, she could speak with a Brooklyn accent when it suited her. She probably learned it from television.

Raina's lips twitched, and she bit her inner cheek to keep from laughing out loud. She would love to see the silver-haired, petite granny bust a karate kick at her burly brother-in-law.

Blue lifted the sledgehammer like it weighed nothing and swung it at the drywall. Instead of punching another grapefruit-size hole into the material, the entire sheet of drywall popped out like it only had been taped in place instead of nailed.

He stared at the wall in confusion. "What?"

"Careful! The whole panel is coming down," Raina said, dragging her grandma back several more steps until they were clear across the room.

"Grab the hammer," Blue said, holding out the sledgehammer and using his shoulder and hand to bear the drywall up against the framing.

Raina darted over, grabbed the sledgehammer, and jumped back to join her grandma.

Blue used both his hands to slowly lower the piece of drywall to the ground. He dropped it the last few inches from the floor, and it hit the floor with a thud, stirring up a puff of dust.

"What is that?" Po Po said, pointing at a blue tarp-wrapped bundle wedged between the studs of the framing. She stepped closer for an inspection and wrinkled her nose. "Must be a dead animal."

She nudged the bag with a toe of her foot, and the whole thing fell onto the floor with a loud thud. Her grandma jumped back. "Yikes!"

Blue turned ashen, and he pointed a shaky finger at the tarp-wrapped bundle. "Wha...what's that?" His tone came out squeakier than normal.

Raina shifted her gaze to the floor and gasped. The tarp had loosened during the fall to reveal a three-inch gap. And through the opening, she saw the first two joints of a skeletal finger. It pointed straight at her grandma's boots.

She swallowed the bile rising in her throat. A

putrid smell seemed to envelop the room. "Don't touch anything. Let's get out of here and call the police."

Chilly Comforts and Disasters
(Raina Sun #9)
Available now.

ABOUT THE AUTHOR

Anne R. Tan is a USA Today bestselling author. She writes the Raina Sun Mystery series and the Lucy Fong Mystery series. Her humorous cozy mysteries feature Chinese-American amateur sleuths dealing with love, family, and life while solving murders.

Sign up for her newsletter for new release announcement, sales, and exclusive content at http://annertan.com/newsletter/

A NOTE FROM ANNE:

My books are my legacy to my children. Unfortunately, they won't grow up in the San Francisco Bay Area as I did. Without a cultural hub to keep the language and philosophies alive, our family will lose this part of our heritage in one generation. My children will be visitors to this rich culture just like my readers. I hope you'll enjoy your time with Raina Sun and her large dynamic family.

www.ingramcontent.com/pod-product-compliance
Lightning Source LLC
Chambersburg PA
CBHW050344190726
48284CB00007BB/2144